KT-521-925

Everything about this situation was just too uncomfortable.

Evan had caught a waft of Violet's floral perfume the other day and it had invaded his senses, instantly taking him back to that night in the bar.

The night when Violet had drunk too many glasses of wine and virtually propositioned him in the corridor leading to the back exit. The night when he'd had too many whiskies and had no resistance to her in her silver dress and spiked heels, her hair all mussed up on her head.

The feel of her hungry lips on his had made him forget where they were and the consequences of his actions.

Hardly the ideal position for a DPA team leader and a member of his staff.

And the next day it was as if nothing had ever happened. He sometimes wondered if Violet even remembered.

Surely she hadn't been that drunk? Because that thought made him sick to his stomach. That would mean he'd taken advantage of her. Something he would never do.

But in the meantime her floral scent lingered around him.

How could he sleep in a room tonight with that aroma and all it conjured up in his mind?

There was no question about it.

Violet Connelly was going to drive him crazy.

Dear Reader

This is the second story in my duet, *Rebels with a Cause*, set around my Disease Prevention Agency. This story looks at another aspect of the DPA and their international role in the fight against polio—a disease that is the subject of a global eradication programme.

Violet Connelly has her own reasons for wanting to be part of the programme. After hiding away for the last three years at a desk job, she feels the time is right to get back out there. Evan Hunter isn't so sure. He's already worked with Violet in the DPA and knows she's hiding something. But is here, the heart of Africa, the place to find out what's been stopping her from forming relationships with those around her and, more importantly, him?

There are some serious issues at the centre of this story. Stillbirth is a very sensitive issue—particularly for Violet, as her circumstances mean she hasn't shared with her family what has happened to her. And Evan already has issues with Violet's brother.

The bad blood between Evan and Sawyer is one of the key linking elements of these stories. Evan was in charge of the mission where Sawyer's wife died. Neither of them has ever spoken about it, but now, with Violet at the heart of things, it's time for them to resolve their issues.

Because—as we all know in the world of Harlequin Mills & Boon®—everyone deserves a Happy Ever After!

Please feel free to contact me via my website and let me know what you think of these stories: www.scarlet-wilson.com. I love to hear from readers!

Scarlet

The first book in Scarlet Wilson's *Rebels with a Cause* duet
THE MAVERICK DOCTOR AND MISS PRIM
is also available this month
from Mills & Boon® Medical Romance™

ABOUT THAT NIGHT...

BY
SCARLET WILSON

First published in Great Britain 2013
by Mills & Boon, an imprint of Harlequin (UK) Limited,
Large Print edition 2014
Eton House, 18-24 Paradise Road,
Richmond, Surrey, TW9 1SR

© 2013 Scarlet Wilson

ISBN: 978 0 263 23857 0

Harlequin (UK) Limited's policy is to use papers that are natural, renewable and recyclable products and made from wood grown in sustainable forests. The logging and manufacturing processes conform to the legal environmental regulations of the country of origin.

Printed and bound in Great Britain
by CPI Antony Rowe, Chippenham, Wiltshire

Scarlet Wilson wrote her first story aged eight and has never stopped. Her family have fond memories of *Shirley and the Magic Purse*, with its army of mice, all with names beginning with the letter 'M'. An avid reader, Scarlet started with every Enid Blyton book, moved on to the *Chalet School* series, and many years later found Mills & Boon®.

She trained and worked as a nurse and health visitor, and currently works in public health. For her, finding Mills & Boon® Medical Romances™ was a match made in heaven. She is delighted to find herself among the authors she has read for many years.

Scarlet lives on the West Coast of Scotland with her fiancé and their two sons.

Recent titles by the same author:

AN INESCAPABLE TEMPTATION
HER CHRISTMAS EVE DIAMOND
A BOND BETWEEN STRANGERS*
WEST WING TO MATERNITY WING!
THE BOY WHO MADE THEM LOVE AGAIN
IT STARTED WITH A PREGNANCY

*The Most Precious Bundle of All

These books are also available in eBook format from www.millsandboon.co.uk

Dedication

In my late teens and early twenties
I had the most fabulous group of friends.
We've all grown older, maybe a little wiser,
and families and continents keep us apart.

So, to the nights in the Metro, Sullivans,
Club de Mar and Ayr Beach Promenade with
Julie Paton, Gillian Lapsley, Joyce Kane, Jaki Lynch,
Shona Kennedy and Marianne Stevenson. I've never
laughed so much. Whose turn is it to drive?

And to @stephenfry, @justinpollard
and the lovely elves at QI
who gave me sleeping sickness just when I needed it!

CHAPTER ONE

VIOLET WAS SHAKING in her shoes—literally.

The walk to the director's office had never seemed so long. On every one of the thirty steps her legs felt more like jelly and her brain like laundry on a permanent spin cycle.

Her hand gripped the piece of paper in her hand tightly—the only evidence that she'd actually done any of the work she was supposed to have completed days ago. The three sentences didn't exactly help her defense.

But inside her, next to her churning stomach, rage was building. Rage against Evan Hunter, her boss.

It was his fault she was in this situation.

He'd asked her to find out background information on her brother, Matt Sawyer, who'd been at the heart of the most prolific outbreak in the history of the Disease Prevention Agency. Granted he hadn't known Matt was her brother, but that did nothing to quell the anger in her belly.

She'd used her other work as an excuse not to comply with Evan's request. Plotting the potential spread of the suspected smallpox virus was surely more important than finding out about the ex-DPA doctor who'd made the preliminary diagnosis. Too bad Evan didn't feel that way.

Her legs trembled as she reached the door.

Stay calm, she repeated in her head. Erupting in front of the director would do nothing to help her cause.

But there was a surprise. Evan's broad shoulders immediately towered over her. It seemed like he was waiting for the director too.

There he was. Blocking her way to the boardroom. His arms were folded across his chest. In another world she might have found him attractive.

In fact, a few months ago and after a couple of glasses of wine, she *had* found him attractive and had ended up locked in a heated embrace that neither of them had admitted to or acted on again.

Evan could certainly turn heads. His tall frame and broad shoulders, combined with his dark brown hair and blue eyes, attracted female attention wherever he went.

To say nothing of the sexy three-day stubble currently on his chin.

Too bad he was about to be her executioner.

So why did he look a little twitchy?

"What are you doing here?"

She jerked at the tone in his voice. "I could ask the same of you. The director sent for me."

"He did?" Evan looked surprised. Surely he'd initiated this by complaining about her?

"Why do you think we're here?"

Evan's eyes met hers. They were steady, uncompromising. "I can only guess it's about the report I sent him."

She could feel her stomach turn over. "What report was that?"

"The one about Matt Sawyer—you know? The one I asked you to write days ago." He shot her a steely glare. "It seemed a remarkable coincidence that a former DPA employee was around when a provisional smallpox diagnosis was made." It was almost as if he was trying to bait her.

"What's the supposed to mean?" The words were out before she could stop herself.

"Oh, come on, Violet." His words were frustrated. "You must appreciate that the chances of smallpox occurring naturally are virtually impossible. All situations in our current plan are around a terrorist attack. What are the chances of a former DPA employee being around when it happens? You were asked to compile a report of Matt Sawyer's recent history. It was essential that we found out exactly where Matt Sawyer had been and who he'd been consorting with."

Violet couldn't hold her tongue any longer. "Consorting with? You've got to be joking, Evan."

But he continued as if she hadn't spoken. "You ignored my requests for information—even after I gave you a warning. That information could have meant the difference between preventing a terrorist attack and putting more lives at risk. You still haven't handed over any information on Matt Sawyer. What exactly have you been doing with your time, Violet?"

The rage that had been simmering beneath the surface was threatening to erupt. Idiot. The man was clearly an idiot. And the implication in his words meant she couldn't think straight any more.

"You honestly thought that Sawyer was a terrorist? That idea actually crossed your tiny, warped mind? You have absolutely no idea what you're talking about. How dare you?" Her voice was rising in crescendo and in pitch.

Evan towered over her. He was furious. "How dare I? I was the lead on this investigation. It was up to me to cover every eventuality—including the possibility of terrorism. How dare *you*, Violet? How dare you obstruct me?"

But Violet wasn't even listening to the words he was saying. She was still stuck on the ridiculous thought that her brother was even remotely connected with this. "I can't believe you thought Sawyer was a terrorist. I can't believe you considered he'd have anything to do with the outbreak. The last thing Sawyer wanted was to be involved with the DPA again. I've never heard anything so ridiculous in my life."

Evan stepped closer. A dark expression swept across his face. "What is it with you and Sawyer, anyway? How do you even know him? He left long before you even got here." His face was only inches from hers. "Why should you have any loyalty to him? What was he—your lover?"

What kind of a question was that? And what was it to him, anyway? Was he jealous?

"What?" The red mist was descending. She couldn't even see his scrunched-up angry face any more. "He's my brother, you idiot!"

There was a hiss. A sharp intake of breath. Evan jerked back as if she'd just delivered an electric shock.

"Your brother?" His voice was barely audible and he looked horrified. "But how can he be your brother?"

Her heart was thudding against her chest wall. Oh, no. She'd just revealed the secret that she'd kept for the past three years.

She couldn't think of anything sensible or rational to say. But, then, Evan had just asked a pretty stupid question. "The same way anyone can be someone's brother," she murmured.

But that clearly wasn't enough for Evan. He hadn't finished with her.

"Sawyer is your brother?" His voice had started to rise.

She nodded. But it obviously wasn't sinking in for him.

"Sawyer is your brother? How can that be possible? You have different names—and you're not married."

Her brain was starting to work in another direction. She had deliberately kept this a secret. Could it be considered fraud? There hadn't been anywhere on her application form to state if family members worked at the DPA. But, then, there would have been an expectation of disclosure. Would she get in trouble for this?

She took a deep breath. "Yes, Matt Sawyer is my brother. I'm well aware that he left here under a cloud and thought it best not to mention our connection. We have different surnames because our mother remarried when I was young. I took my stepfather's surname—Matt didn't."

She held the crumpled piece of paper up in her hand, trying to ignore the fact that it was shaking. "As I'm sure you were aware, Matt hasn't made much contact over the past few years. He struggled with Helen's death. I've never known where he's been working. It turns out he's been in Borneo, Alaska and Connecticut." She hesitated. Should she say any more? "And I never found that out for myself. I've been trying to find out where my brother's been for years. Matt told me and I checked the details."

Evan erupted. "Why on earth didn't you tell me he was your brother? I asked you to investigate him and you said nothing! You had a conflict of interest that you should have declared. Of all the unprofessional—"

Violet flinched and stepped forward instantly, her face inches from his. "Unprofessional? Well, let's talk about unprofessional behavior, shall we? Because I'm not the only one to indulge in that. I'm not the only one keeping secrets around here."

"Ahem."

The loud noise of someone clearing their throat made them both jump.

The director was standing behind them both with a pile of papers in his arms, looking less than impressed. He pushed open the door to the boardroom. "Let's take this inside, please, and stop entertaining the masses." How much had he heard?

Violet's jaw dropped and her head shot round to the office space where just about every member of staff was standing on their feet, their heads above their cubicle walls, staring at her and Evan.

How long had they been like this? And why hadn't she noticed? She felt heat flood into her cheeks and hurried into the boardroom behind the director.

She couldn't breathe. She couldn't think. All the nerves that she'd felt a few minutes ago on the walk to the boardroom instantly returned.

The director seemed cool and unfazed. He walked around the desk and sat down in his chair. He placed his paperwork in front of him and gestured to the chairs on the other side of the desk. "Take a seat please. Violet, Evan."

What was that paperwork? Was that the HR documentation he needed to fire her?

She swallowed. A tennis ball was sitting in her throat. *Just get this over with.*

There was a few minutes' silence as the director looked at the paperwork in front of him. It was agonizing. The wait seemed to stretch on and on for ever. She couldn't stand it.

Evan obviously couldn't either. "Director, if you'll just let me explain—"

The director held up one hand. "Enough."

Evan tried to speak again, his face flushed. "But—"

"From both of you." The director's voice cut him dead. He pulled some papers out from the file in front of him.

Violet felt her chest tightening and she struggled to breathe. Was this it? Was she about to get fired?

The director looked her in the eye. He had pale grey eyes. She'd never really noticed before. She'd always been too busy keeping her head down and stopping herself being noticed.

"Dr. Connelly."

She gulped. He was addressing her formally. This couldn't be good.

He sighed. "Putting aside what I just witnessed outside, I actually came here today to let you know that your transfer request has been approved."

"What?"

"What?"

Their voices rang out simultaneously, as if neither of them could really believe their ears.

He folded his hands in front of him. "But with

hindsight it seems as if there are a number of issues we need to address here today."

"Transfer request? What transfer request?"

Evan's head was spinning. He'd had no idea
why he'd been called to the boardroom. He'd as-
sumed it was regarding the missing report. The
report on her brother.

Now it seemed as if the director hadn't even
noticed the report *was* missing.

The director shot him another steely glare.
He obviously didn't like to be interrupted. "Dr.
Connelly had requested to be transferred to the
emergency operations center and join the stop
transmission of polio program."

His brain whirred. Violet Connelly had been
driving him crazy for months. Ever since they'd
kissed on that night out and both of them had
pretended it hadn't happened.

But the issues in the past few days had been
serious. Serious enough for him to consider reporting her. No matter what their history was.
As team leader he had a responsibility to ensure
everyone pulled their weight.

Since when had Violet wanted to do field work?
And why had she never mentioned it?

"I had no idea. She obviously didn't see fit to mention it to me." The hard edge in his voice was crystal clear and he could hear the way his words must sound to her—cold.

Did that hide the fact he couldn't explain how he was feeling?

Was Violet leaving because of him? Was she leaving because of their mistaken, fumbled kiss?

And why did the thought of not seeing her any more drive him just as crazy as working with her every day?

He watched as she seemed to sag into her chair. As if all the tension had just left her body. Disbelief was written all over her face.

"Really? You've approved my transfer? When can I start? Where am I going? What will my role be?" It was obvious her mouth was running away with her and her brain had gone into overdrive.

Meanwhile, he was still getting over the shock that he wouldn't be seeing Violet anymore. It almost squeezed the air from his lungs.

"Hold on." The director raised his hands. "I think there are bigger issues here." He looked between the two of them and leaned back in his chair. "I have to say that I'm disappointed in you both." Evan felt his heart sink like a stone. This couldn't be good.

"Evan, I'm surprised that Dr. Connelly didn't tell you about her application to transfer. As her line manager I would have expected you both to have discussed this." The implication was clear. Why couldn't Violet speak to him? He kind of wondered that himself. Was he really so unapproachable?

"And Dr. Connelly..." He turned his head back to Violet. "Unlike Dr. Hunter, I don't really care that Matt Sawyer is your brother. I can't think why you thought it necessary to hide that, but I'm very happy with the work your brother has done over the past few days for us. And I'll be keen to work with him again in the future." He tapped his pen against the desk, as if he was contemplating what to say next.

"It's my opinion that your reaction to Dr. Hunter was unreasonable. He was just exploring every angle regarding the possibility of a smallpox outbreak. We would have checked up on anyone who reported a suspected outbreak, no matter who they were. But what's clear to me is that Dr. Hunter didn't explain his rationale for his request very well. But then again, why should he? He was in charge of the team."

Evan had no idea where this was going. He could see Violet struggling to swallow. She was finding this as difficult as he was. One second he'd thought the director was going to come down on Violet, and the next second he thought his own head was going to be on the chopping block.

Something struck him. *Was.* The director had said he *was* in charge of the team. Oh, no.

Violet's face had fallen again. And he hated it when she looked like that. One minute she was getting her dream transfer the next she was thinking she was being given her marching orders.

"What's most clear to me here is that the two of you need to learn to work together as a team. I don't care what your personal issues are. What I do care about is how the staff at the DPA work together. It's one of the most vital components of our jobs." His eyes narrowed, "And the display I've just witnessed gives me great concern."

He turned on Evan. "You're one of my most experienced and senior doctors. I would expect better from you. The exchange outside seemed unprofessional."

This was it. He was going to be fired.

Unprofessional.

The word that he and Violet had just flung at each other. Hearing it come from the director's mouth was an entirely different matter.

It was the most offensive word you could say to a doctor. Particularly when it hit home.

"You are two of the best clinically competent doctors that I have and it's time to put your skills to good use. So I've come to a decision. Violet, you will be joining the polio team in Nigeria. I've already approved the transfer. They are on the final push to try and stop the spread of polio. Your field assignment will last three months and you'll be leaving in a week. Start packing."

Evan swallowed nervously as the director turned to face him. "Evan, I think it's time for a change of scene for you. And maybe a change of climate. I'm happy with the way you handled the potential outbreak. I'm even happier that it turned out to be monkeypox instead of smallpox, but I think it's time you learned a different skill set.

"I've had no complaints about you—no complaints at all. I am conscious, though, that working in the same area of the DPA can make a doctor complacent. I need adaptable team leaders who can work anywhere, covering every eventuality. You need to work on your interpersonal skills. Specifically, your interpersonal skills with Violet."

He tilted his head to one side, almost as if he was lost in thought for a moment. "I think, at times, you can be a little hard on your team." A smile drifted across his face, "A little too alpha. I need a team leader for the polio program at short notice and was struggling to find someone appropriate—someone who could take care of the strategic work alongside the clinical. It seems like I've just found him."

"Me?" Evan could hardly get the word out. This couldn't be happening. This was like a bad movie.

The director nodded. "That's why I was late for our meeting. I was taking a call from Africa. One of our team leaders needs to get back home in a hurry—his father has been taken seriously ill. I'm sure you understand." The words hung in the air—along with the implication.

What a terrible position. There was no way Evan could say no now.

The director gave him a little nod. "You'll be assigned to work with a national counterpart. The Healthly World Federation and Global Children's Support Organization are our partners in this area. You'll have to plan, implement, roll out and monitor the program in your designated area.

"You'll have to manage a team of civilians and train them to help administer the program." He almost gave a little smile. "That will take all your people powers. You'll have to learn to be flexible, working under difficult conditions with people from different cultures." He gave a curt nod. "It could be the making of you, Evan."

The director was moving now, picking up his paperwork. He glanced from one to the other. "Maybe three months in a hot climate will help you two sort out your differences."

The realization of what was about to happen hit him like a boulder on the head. "We're going together? To Nigeria? I'm going to be *Dr. Connelly's* team leader?"

He couldn't possibly mean that. From the little Evan knew about the polio program it worked across a number of countries. Surely, the director didn't plan on sending them together on the same field assignment?

"Of course. This is perfect. Hard work in an area uncluttered by other distractions. The two of you are there to represent the clinical expertise of the DPA, so I expect you to iron out any personal issues. Both of you report to Dr. Sanday tomorrow morning. He'll give you all the background information and travel arrangements that you need."

"But what about here? What about infectious diseases?"

The director gave him a wry smile. "Donovan's served his time well. I think he's ready to take the next step—a more strategic direction. It will stretch him, do him good—just like it will you."

And then he was gone.

Violet sat in the chair, unmoving. Evan could almost sense she didn't want to meet his gaze.

There was so much going on in his head right now. And most of it concerned her. She was shifting constantly in his mind. Violet, Sawyer's sister. Violet, his colleague who'd ignored his instructions. Violet, the woman he'd kissed a few months ago. Violet, the woman who'd asked for a transfer without talking to him first.

Violet, the woman he was going to spend the next three months with—in close proximity.

Was that better or worse than her leaving? Right now he didn't know.

It didn't help matters that he was being replaced by a guy he considered a cocky upstart.

"Are you going to say something?" She'd rested her elbow on the desk and was leaning her head on her hand. She looked exhausted.

Then again, she'd barely slept in the past few days. None of them had, thanks to the crisis.

Her eyes were closed. For the first time he noticed she had little dark circles under them. They marred her usually perfect complexion. Her blond hair was swept back with a clip but little strands had escaped around her face. Even in a state of exhaustion Violet Connelly was a thing of beauty.

But her beauty couldn't distract him from the thoughts rattling around in his brain.

"Why didn't you tell me about Sawyer? No. Why didn't you tell *anyone* that he's your brother? Are you ashamed of him?"

Her eyes shot open, sparks of fury shooting in his direction. She opened her mouth to speak then pressed her lips together firmly for a few seconds, obviously having second thoughts. Maybe she'd been outspoken enough for one day. She bent forward, putting her head on the desk in exasperation.

"You do that to me," she mumbled.

He was thrown. "What?"

She lifted her head, so he could only see one pale green eye. "You make me mad at the drop of a hat. It irritates me. And I'm just too exhausted to fight with you."

He nodded slowly. This wasn't exactly where he thought this conversation would go.

"Of course I'm not ashamed of my brother. I love him dearly. But he's had issues. He needed time. He needed space. Ever heard of the expression *'If you love someone let them go'*? That's Sawyer. The past six years have been hard." Her pale green eyes looked off to the side and she nodded slowly. "But I think he's on his way back."

Wow. Nothing like getting to the heart of the

matter. But he didn't have time to think about what she'd said because she wasn't finished.

"But I don't know where you fit into this picture."

"What do you mean?" Her conversation seemed to jump all over the place. What was going on in her mind? Was this lack of sleep?

She folded her arms across her chest and straightened herself in the chair.

"I know you had issues with my brother but I don't know what they were. Sawyer never told me. Will you?"

Now, there was a question. The words hung in the air. Could he really put into words the complexity of what had happened between him and Sawyer and how he felt? He almost didn't know where to start. And did he really want to have this conversation with a woman he would spend the next three months with? The answer was easy.

"Probably not."

She sucked in a deep breath. "Well, where does that leave us?"

"What do you mean?"

"Does your irrational hatred of my brother extend to me too?"

He swallowed, not really sure how to answer. The truth of the matter was that it did change how he perceived her. His bias against Sawyer was already affecting how he felt about her. Would she exhibit the same traits as her brother? Would she walk out on a mission when it was at its most vital stage?

He set his lips in a firm line but he couldn't look at her and his voice was low. "You know I don't hate you, Violet." His brain was painting pictures. Pictures of Violet in that red dress she'd been wearing a few days ago with a thick black belt cinching her waist. He was sure she'd worn it to distract him from the fact she hadn't produced the report. And she had been right to, because it had worked.

Her eyes drifted off to one side. "I thought I was going to get fired."

He nodded slowly. "Me too."

Her green eyes met his. "I don't want to get fired," she said steadily. "I love my job."

"I don't want to get fired either. My job's the best thing in my life right now."

Why had he said that?

That was far too personal. And Evan tried not

to mix his personal life and with his working life. Or, at least, not usually.

"So I guess we both have to make the best of the situation."

She didn't acknowledge his words. Instead, she pulled out a flower-covered notebook and started scribbling.

"What are you doing?"

"I need to make plans. I need to make arrangements for my apartment. The electricity, the rent, the mail…" Her voice tailed off.

The enormity of the upheaval started to hit him too. He'd need to make similar plans—all in the space of a week. To say nothing of the handover he'd have to give to Donovan about running the team here. The next week would be a nightmare.

Violet was scribbling again. It was almost as if he wasn't there. He watched her as her hand flew over the page. Her hair was falling over her face. His fingers itched to reach out and tuck it behind her ear. Why on earth did he think like this around her?

"Any chance of a copy of your list? It will save me doing mine."

She raised her head and the sides of her mouth

turned up. "Not a hope." She stood up and walked toward the door. "I'm going to start going over my files, see what work I need to hand over to someone else."

"Violet?"

She stopped, her hand on the doorhandle. "What?"

He couldn't help it. He had to ask. Did she have the same kind of traits that he'd seen in her brother? He needed to know. The next three months were going to be a strain. Ever since that kiss he'd spent the past few months avoiding being in close proximity to her.

They'd never spoken about it. Never mentioned it. A drunken fumble on a work night out that no one knew about.

He had no idea how she felt about it.

More importantly, he'd no idea how *he* felt about it.

He'd woken up the next morning with the strangest feeling in his stomach. Part dread, part excitement. He was her boss. He should never have gone near her. It compromised their working relationship.

And now it seemed as if she was prepared to

hold it over his head. That made Violet dangerous. That made Violet a threat.

"When the director interrupted us you were
saying something about me being unprofessional.
You were implying that because of the kiss. You
thought you were about to be fired. Were you
going to try and get me fired too? Would you do
that, Violet?"

Her eyes met his and he saw a little flash of
fire. She didn't hesitate for a second. "In a heartbeat."

She pushed open the door and walked out, leaving Evan wondering what he'd got himself into.

CHAPTER TWO

THE HEAT HIT her as soon as they stepped off the plane. It was like stepping into a fan-heated oven.

How on earth could she function in this for the next three months? Would she ever get used to it?

The sweat was already starting to run in rivulets down her back and catch in her bra strap. She rummaged in her bag and pulled out a travel-sized antiperspirant spray. "I'm heading to the ladies' room. Can you watch for my bag? It's lime-green."

Evan nodded and dropped his rucksack onto the floor beside the luggage carousel. Great. A twelve-hour flight from Atlanta to Lagos, Nigeria, and he still wasn't speaking to her.

Not that she cared. But it was unnerving to sit next to someone for that long without exchanging a single word.

She splashed some water on her face and pulled a ponytail band from her bag, sweeping her sticky hair from the back of her neck. She pulled off her white top and sprayed liberally before swapping it for a purple one in her rucksack. It was a little crumpled but it would have to do.

Was Evan planning on speaking to her any time soon? And what did he have to be so mad about, anyway? She'd only told him the truth. And if he couldn't handle the truth...

She heard the squeak of luggage being wheeled past the doorway. People were obviously leaving so the baggage must have arrived.

She picked up her bag and headed back outside, just in time to see Evan drag her lime-green suitcase from the carousel.

It landed with a thump at her feet. "What on earth have you got in here? Did you pack the entire contents of your apartment? I've never seen a suitcase that size in my life. As for the weight, how on earth did you get it down your stairs?"

She watched as he pulled another suitcase—this time with one hand—from the carousel. It was a medium-sized navy blue case. She couldn't help the smile that flickered across her lips.

She tilted her head up at him. "Oh, so now you're talking to me, are you?" She pulled the handle up on the side of her case and tilted it onto its wheels. The initial tug was tough but once the case picked up a little momentum, it sailed along behind her.

"Do you remember the name of the person we're meeting?" She walked in the direction of the exit.

Evan was matching her stride for stride, holding his case easily in his hand—he had no need for wheels. He pulled a piece of paper from his top pocket. "Someone called Amos should be waiting for us outside Arrivals with a car. They said under no circumstances should we get in a local taxi." His eyes fell on her suitcase again. "Though at this rate we'll probably need an eighteen-wheeler to move that. What do you have in there?"

Violet rolled her eyes. "Just everything a girl could need. Hold up a sec," she said, as one of the customs officers gestured toward her.

Two hours later they finally made it to the exit.

"Of all the ridiculous, over-packed, stupid items to have in your suitcase—"

"Oh, drop it, Evan. I'm too hot and tired to listen to your whining." She nodded in the direction of a man with a board showing their names in his hand. He looked as if he was wilting.

"Hi," she said. "Amos? I'm Violet Connelly and this is Evan Hunter. Sorry we took so long."

The man's brow furrowed. "Was there a problem with the officials? I hope not."

Evan let out a snort. "The only problems were the ones that she caused. Probably by trying to transport the equivalent of an elephant in her luggage."

"An elephant? I don't understand."

Violet placed her hand over his. "Dr. Hunter is being sarcastic. The officials searched my luggage and removed certain items."

"Items? What items?"

Violet shook her head. "Nothing important. Some U.S. candy. Some electrical items. Nothing I can't live without."

Evan was obviously becoming impatient. The two-hour-long inspection of Violet's luggage must have been the final straw for him. "Do you have a car?"

Amos nodded. "The minibus is parked outside. I'll take you to the Healthy World Federation building and give you some safety instructions.

Stay next to me, please, as we leave the building. Some of the local taxis will try and encourage you to go with them."

He grabbed hold of the handle of Violet's case and stopped dead, obviously unprepared for the weight. He struggled to give her a smile as he dragged it along behind him. Within a few minutes they were outside the terminal building and were immediately accosted by a whole host of taxi drivers.

"Stay close!" shouted Amos as they pushed their way through. Evan's hand appeared from nowhere and rested gently at her waist, guiding her through the shouting faces until they reached the car park.

"How far to the city?"

The long flight, followed by the search at customs, had taken their toll. Violet was ready to collapse in a heap. "Around fifty minutes. We're just going to the outskirts. It's a relatively safe area. Don't worry."

He opened the back door of the minibus and nodded to Evan. "Give us a hand with this, please." Evan grabbed the other side of the case and between them they tossed it into the back of the minivan. Maybe a big suitcase hadn't been such a good idea after all. But at the time she'd been packing everything had seemed like an essential.

The journey flew past. Violet could barely keep her eyes open as they sped through the city suburbs. It was immediately apparent that poverty was an issue—just like in so many other cities throughout the world.

She felt a sharp nudge on the ribs. "Wake up, Violet, we're here."

Her eyes shot open. When had she fallen asleep? The last thing she remembered was staring out the window at a group of children playing football in the street.

Somehow she'd fallen asleep with her head on Evan's shoulder, and the heat from his body in the air-conditioned van had been comforting. She pulled herself up straight and rubbed at her cheek. Great. She could feel the creases of his shirt embedded in her face.

She looked out the window as Amos opened the door and let the heat flood inside again.

She'd had a little handheld, battery-powered

fan in her suitcase. Too bad she hadn't thought to put it in her hand luggage.

She jumped down onto the street and immediately pulled her sunglasses down from her forehead. She glanced at her watch. It was still set to Atlanta time. Lagos was only five hours ahead, but the jump between time zones had totally disorientated her. It felt as if it should be the middle of the night.

Amos hauled her case up the front steps of the building and pushed open the glass doors. Air-conditioning again. Bliss.

A woman in traditional dress met them at reception. "Dr. Hunter? Dr. Connelly? Welcome to headquarters." She gestured toward the rear of the building. "If you want to head to the lifts, I'll give you a key to your rooms. You'll have a chance to freshen up, but we need you back down here later to meet the members of your team and have a safety briefing."

"No problem." Evan obviously wasn't suffering from the same travel effects that she was. Right now she just wanted to lie down on some cool cotton sheets.

Evan glanced at the number of the key and

pocketed it. Both of them stood for a few more seconds, waiting for the second key to appear.

It didn't.

The lady looked back up. "Oh, didn't someone explain? We're a little short of space. You'll be bunking up together. That won't be a problem, will it?"

Her manner was so relaxed it almost disarmed Violet. What Violet really wanted to do was scream and shout and stamp her feet on the floor. Her patience and fatigue was at an all-time low.

"No problem at all." Evan's cool voice cut through the strop she was currently throwing in her head and he headed off toward the lift.

She bit her tongue and tugged her case after him, struggling to pull it over the seam between the floor and elevator door. Evan's hand slid over hers and he gave it a final tug, sending her hurtling backward into the lift. She landed against the back wall with a thud.

"Thanks." She couldn't hide her sarcastic tone and wasn't even going to try.

"My pleasure." She could hear the edge of amusement in his voice and she really wasn't in the mood at all.

He pressed a button and the elevator slid smoothly upward, opening onto a brightly lit corridor with a procession of identical brown doors.

"Can you manage?"

"Of course." She tugged her case with both hands, smiling as his foot came into contact with one of the wheels. It really did feel as if she had a dead body inside.

He flinched. "We're in here." He slid the card into the door and pushed it open, revealing a regular-sized room with a large white bed.

One large white bed.

Silence.

Who would react first?

It was Violet. It was the final straw.

"You have got to be joking!"

Evan's eyes swept the room, obviously looking for somewhere else to sleep. No stowaway bed. No pull-down couch.

One bed. Or nothing.

Violet stomped over to the bathroom and stuck her head inside. Clean. Functional. White bath and a separate shower.

"What are you looking for, a secret bed?"

His voice made her jump, his warm breath tickling the hairs at the back of her neck. She spun round. "Don't do that!"

He smiled and it caught her unawares. The sun was streaming through the window, lighting up his face. When had been the last time she'd seen him smile? She couldn't remember.

One thing was for sure. Evan Hunter should smile more often.

There were little lines around his blue eyes but they didn't detract from how handsome he was. They only added character. And he was so close she could see little flecks of gold in them.

She was so tired right now. All she wanted to do was lean forward, bury her head in his firm chest and go to sleep. The bed in the middle of the room was practically shouting her name. But there was no way they could share a bed.

Especially after what had happened a few months ago.

The kiss had been steamy enough. But the two of them in a bed?

No. The picture that was conjuring up in her brain was too much. This fatigue was stopping any rational thoughts whatsoever.

Evan folded his arms across his chest.

"I don't know about you, Violet, but I have no intention of sleeping on the floor."

He was right. She knew he was right.

She glanced around at the floor. There wasn't even as much as a rug to lie on.

Sharing a room in close proximity to Evan would be hard enough. But sharing a bed? It didn't even bear thinking about.

There was a small table and chairs in front of the window in the room.

"How about we sleep in shifts?" She moved quickly, crossing the room in strides and jumping onto the bed. "I'll go first."

Her head sank instantly into the pillow. Perfect. She didn't care what he thought. She needed to get some sleep. Now.

Evan sat down on one of the chairs, leaning forward and pulling a thick wad of papers from the zipped pocket in his case. His eyes ran over her body as she shuffled her shoes off and kicked them to the floor. Was he looking at her curves? Was he thinking about the last time he'd had his hands on her body?

That sent a whole new sensation prickling across her skin.

"Cranky when you're tired, aren't you? Fine. You sleep. I'll read. I'll wake you up in a few hours, in time for the briefing. Okay?"

"Okay," she said instantly. There was no way she was getting off this comfortable bed.

How bad could this be? Maybe in a few hours they would be able to find someone else to share with?

Her eyes flickered shut.

She and Evan Hunter in a shared room.

Not the best start to her new life. Three years ago she'd originally applied to be part of this program but circumstances had changed and the thought of mainstream clinical work—potentially with lots of children—had been too difficult for her.

It hadn't helped that her grieving brother hadn't been in touch. Neither were her parents. They still hadn't recovered from the loss of their daughter-in-law and first grandchild some years earlier. Telling them about her own circumstances would only have added to their pain. And they hadn't needed that.

So she'd gone through everything herself.

Oh, she'd had some good friends who'd been

there for her but it wasn't the same as family, no matter how much she tried to spin it in her mind.

But life had come full circle. Time was supposed to be a great healer.

Maybe it was. Maybe it wasn't.

She was ready for a change. She was a doctor. She'd spent the past three years in the epidemiology and planning department of the DPA.

It had been fine—for a desk job. But Violet was a people person.

The conflict—and incursion—with Evan Hunter had given her the impetus she needed to apply for a transfer. She wanted to have contact with patients again. She wanted to help people. She wanted to make a difference.

And out here, in Nigeria, she could certainly help to make a difference with the polio program.

It was time to get back out into the real world. And you didn't get much more real than the heart of Africa.

She had her mind set on this. Getting involved again. Having contact with families. Having contact with mothers. Having contact with children. Having contact with babies.

Evan Hunter was nothing more than an inconvenience.

A handsome inconvenience.

She had work to do here, and he'd better not
get in her way.

She snuggled further into the pillow and prayed
she didn't snore.

Evan gave her shoulder a little shake again, raising his voice just a little. "Violet. Violet. It's time
to wake up. We've got the briefing in half an
hour."

She stirred and mumbled something. It almost
felt unfair to wake her. She was much nicer while
she slept.

Less distracting. Less confrontational. Less a
reminder of her brother.

He still hadn't got over that. Matt Sawyer's sister. Wow. He hadn't seen that one coming. Not
by a long shot.

She was mumbling again. She'd spent the past
few hours doing that. Talking in her sleep. It was
kind of cute. Not that he thought Violet was cute.

Not at all.

Plus, he didn't have a single clue what she'd

been saying. At one point it had almost sounded like someone's name.

Her eyes flickered open and took a few moments to focus. At the exact moment a drip from his still-wet hair landed on her nose. He'd taken the opportunity to shower while she'd been sleeping and hadn't got round to rubbing his hair with a towel.

"Eeeewwww!" She sat up sharply, her hand automatically rubbing her nose.

"Sorry."

She glanced at her watch then screwed up her nose. "What time is it here? I'm still on Atlanta time."

"It's nearly six o'clock. You'd better get ready. I thought you might want to shower."

She pushed herself up the bed. "Have you left any hot water?"

He shrugged. "You know what they say—if you're not fast, you're last."

A pillow sailed from the bed and caught him on the side of his head. "Hey!"

Her head turned to the side, taking in the table where he'd been sitting. The papers and documentation had spilled over onto the other chair and across half the floor.

"Did you kill half a tree while I was sleeping?" She walked over and picked up some of the paperwork. "Do we really need to read all this?"

He shook his head. "You don't. I do. You only need to read around half."

She seemed to gulp. "Wow."

She gave her eyes a little rub. "I think I will shower." She tipped her case over and opened it up.

She hadn't been joking. She really did have everything—despite having had some things removed at the airport. But what was more interesting was how everything was packed. Rolled-up tiny items, all in blocks of color. Nothing like the flat-folded items in his case. She even had her toiletries stuffed into her shoes.

She unrolled a light yellow dress, some white underwear and pulled some shampoo from a shoe. "I'll only be five minutes."

And she was. Her hair was still wet but pulled back into a braid that fell straight down her back.

It really was disarming how pretty she could look without even trying.

She picked up a notebook with purple flowers on the front. He squinted. "Are those violets?"

She nodded and smiled. "I have a whole boxful of these at home. Pretty, aren't they? At least no one can steal my signature notebook." The smile reached all the way up to her eyes.

It was nice to see a genuine smile. The past few weeks she'd had a permanent scowl on her face. But maybe that was especially for him. He liked her better this way.

"Did you buy them?"

"No. Sawyer did."

How to break a moment. It was like someone had just thrown a bucket of ice over him.

He just couldn't get past the connection.

He'd been the team leader. The one responsible for all members of staff.

And Sawyer's wife, Helen, had died on that mission. Stuck out in the middle of nowhere with an ectopic pregnancy. By the time they'd recognized what was wrong it had been too late for her.

He blamed Sawyer. He must have known his wife was pregnant and yet he had let her go on that mission.

But Evan also had reason to blame himself, and

six years on he still couldn't get the guilt out of his head. Six years on he still hadn't managed to shake the feeling that he was living a life his colleague wasn't. It didn't seem fair. It wasn't as if he was short of offers. Sure, he dated. But the first time he even felt a flicker of something toward the woman of the moment, they had to go. Because why should he get to live, love and procreate when his colleague didn't?

The sensation of guilt was a hideous, never-ending cycle. Sometimes it faded a little, only to flicker back into life as soon as something sparked a memory.

Violet was ready now, her eyes quizzical as if she had been reading his secret thoughts, her hand on the doorhandle. "Let's go," she said quietly.

He followed her to the elevators and down to the conference room. It was impressive. One wall was covered in maps of the states of Nigeria. Another had organizational charts of the team members. Another had immunization targets and notifications.

Everything they needed was right before their eyes.

"Welcome, Evan. Welcome, Violet. I'm Frank

Barns, director of DPA's Nigeria office." He gestured to the walls. "Welcome to the operations center."

He shook their hands and led them over to the nearest wall where the maps were displayed. "I finished a briefing for the other new staff earlier. You've probably realized we're at a real tipping point with polio eradication. If immunity is not raised in the three remaining countries to levels necessary to stop poliovirus transmission, then polio eradication will fail. Nigeria is the only polio-endemic country remaining in Africa. There are several high-risk states and I've decided to send you to Natumba state. We've had sixty-two cases of wild poliovirus this year—more than half of them notified from Natumba. One third of all children there remain under-immunized."

He gave them a little nod of his head. "You'll have your work cut out for you there. The DPA works in conjunction with The Global Children's Support Organization and the Healthy World Federation. But there are several issues for our workers." His expression was deadly serious. "There have been bomb threats, killings and kidnappings. We have to make security a priority for our staff. You don't go anywhere unescorted. While in Lagos you stay with a local guide, and the same applies when you reach Natumba."

Evan could see Violet's face pale. Was she frightened? Maybe she hadn't been expecting this. He moved next to her and placed his hand over hers. Frank was still talking, outlining the things they should or shouldn't do. He almost expected Violet to snatch her hand away. But she didn't.

Instead she twined her fingers with his, while keeping her breathing slow and steady. She was scared.

And it scared him too. He was going to be team leader again. He was going to be out in the field, with a whole host of unknowns. A whole host of things he might not be able to predict or control.

What if something happened to one of his team again?

The guilt had almost destroyed him last time. What if something happened to Violet? It almost didn't bear thinking about.

He pressed his fingers closer to hers and gave her a little smile while Frank continued with the briefing.

He would keep her safe. He had to.

He couldn't think beyond that.

"Wow. What did you think of all that?"

It was an hour later and they were sitting in the dining room in the HWF building.

"So much for having a last supper before starting on the job." She glanced around at her surroundings. They'd been advised not to leave the building at night, and neither of them had wanted to ignore the security brief.

"It's probably for the best. We've got an early start tomorrow with the flight to Natumba."

He was pushing his food around the plate, his mind obviously on other things.

"So, how do you feel about it?" She felt as if something was caught in her throat. Would he feel the same way she did? Sick with nerves? She hadn't expected this. She hadn't planned for it.

His eyes met hers. And she could almost see the shutters go down. It was apparent he wasn't going to tell her how he was feeling about it all. After all, he hadn't even wanted to come here, had he? He'd been more or less pushed into this.

She'd chosen to come here. She should have

been better prepared for what she was getting into. The briefing today had knocked her for six. Would she even sleep tonight?

Sleep. That other issue.

"Did you manage to get the sleeping arrangements sorted out?" Evan had said he would try and talk to someone about finding another room.

He looked up from his plate, a smile dancing across his lips. "Yes and no."

"What does that mean?"

"It means I've got us some extra pillows."

"And what are they for?"

"To put down the middle of the bed." She almost dropped her fork. They were still sleeping in the same bed? Oh, no.

Her skin was starting to tingle. The hairs on her arms were standing on end. Sharing a bed with Evan Hunter? Pillows or not, she wouldn't sleep a wink.

"You okay with that?"

He seemed so cool. So calm and collected. His mind was obviously focused on the job and not doing a merry dance around the thoughts of a heated kiss a few months ago.

Not the way hers was.

"I'm fine with that." She put her fork down. "I've had enough. I think I want to get to bed early."

She'd said the words. She hadn't meant them to come out sounding like that. Sounding as if she was hinting at something. She wanted to die of embarrassment and felt the rush of blood to her cheeks.

Evan kept his eyes fixed on his dinner plate. He handed over the key to the room. "I'll let you go on ahead. I've got some things to work out with Frank. We'll probably be talking late into the night. Leave the door on the latch. I promise I won't wake you when I come up."

She nodded and just about grabbed the key from his hand, thankful that he seemed to have missed the implication of her words. "Good night, then." She sped off to the room. The sooner she had her head under the covers the better.

This was going to be a long night.

Evan watched her retreating back. In the artificially lit room he could see her silhouette through her thin yellow dress, showing the curve of her bottom and hips. He did his best to look away.

This was all going to end in disaster.

He'd lied. He didn't have to see Frank about anything. He'd been given all the information he could possibly need.

The worst thing was that he'd left all the paperwork in the room. He was going to have to hang around and kill time with nothing to do.

It had seemed easier to make something up. To let her slip away and get to the room without him pretending not to watch her every move.

Leave the door on the latch. He cringed at his words. It was like something an old married couple would say to each other. Where had that come from?

Everything about this situation was just too uncomfortable.

He'd caught a waft of her floral perfume the other day and it had invaded his senses, instantly taking him back to that night in the bar.

The night when Violet had drunk too many glasses of wine and had virtually propositioned him in the corridor leading to the back exit. The night when he'd had too many whiskies and had no resistance to her in her red dress and spiked heels, her hair all mussed up on her head.

The feel of her hungry lips on his had made him forget where they were and the consequences of his actions.

By the time someone had interrupted them, he'd practically had her dress up around her waist.

Hardly the ideal position for a DPA team leader and a member of his staff.

And the next day it had been as if nothing had ever happened. He sometimes wondered if Violet even remembered the incident.

Surely she hadn't been that drunk? Because that thought made him sick to his stomach. That would mean he'd taken advantage of her. Something he would never do.

But in the meantime her floral scent lingered around him.

How could he sleep in a room tonight with that aroma and all it conjured up in his mind?

There was no question about it.

Violet Connelly was going to drive him crazy.

CHAPTER THREE

THE LIGHT AIRCRAFT touched down in a cloud of dust.

"We're here." Violet pressed her nose up against the glass window, trying to take in the wide landscape ahead of her.

Natumba state covered more than eighteen thousand square kilometers, and they'd landed in the northernmost tip, at the three local government areas most affected by polio. Only a few days ago there had been another two diagnoses of wild poliovirus.

Part of her was relieved they weren't going to be based in the capital, Natumba. There was another team already based there.

But the wide open landscape and vast terrain made her realize the huge task they were undertaking and the number of miles they'd need to cover. All in the blistering heat.

There were a few figures dressed in white next

to the landing strip, along with a whole host of multi-terrain vehicles—some looking a little worse for wear.

"That must be Dr. Yusif. He said he would meet us here and take us to the campsite."

"I didn't expect it to be so green. I expected it to look more barren."

Evan turned as he unloaded their bags and all the supplies from the plane. "Natumba is quite an agricultural state—they produce a lot of groundnuts. The land is supposed to be well cultivated and irrigated."

"And the villages?" She left the question hanging in the air between them.

Both of them had read as much as they could about the surrounding area. Only half of the population in the area had access to portable water and appropriate sanitation. Health care was limited and the education system in a state of neglect.

Although the government had launched national campaigns to raise awareness about polio, the reality was the message wasn't reaching the villagers.

"Nigeria isn't all savannah. The far south has

a tropical rainforest climate and good rainfall. There are also areas of saltwater swamp and mangroves. The border with Cameroon has highlands and a rich rainforest. It's not the dry desert wasteland that some people expect."

Dr. Yusif was striding across the ground to meet them. He was dressed in a white shirt and trousers with a white *kufi* cap on his head. "Welcome, welcome." His smile reached from ear to ear. "I'm so glad to see you." He shook hands with them both and guided them over to the vehicles. "Grab your bags and let's get on the move. It will be too hot to travel if we don't start now."

"How far away is the campsite?" Violet asked as she slid into the backseat of the four wheel drive. The upholstery of the seats were ripped and scorched by the sun. She pulled her skirt down to stop her skin from sticking to the surface. It must be around one hundred degrees in here, nothing like the comfortable, air-conditioned vehicles they'd had in the city, or that she took for granted back home.

"It's only around an hour, but the roads can be rough. Hold on to your hat!"

Evan slid in next to her and they listened as Dr.

Yusif filled them in on some of the background to where they'd be working. Violet clung onto the grab handle on the roof as the car pitched over the uneven terrain—anything to stop her sliding across the seat and landing in Evan's lap.

He was managing to look as cool and calm as ever. How did he do it? The sweat was already starting to trickle down her spine and she was wishing she had pulled her hair off her collar with an elastic band.

Dr. Yusif seemed to talk constantly. It seemed that he'd been here, without support, for some time and was relieved that they'd arrived. He was moving on to another area and would introduce them to the team covering the three local areas, which Evan would be leading.

Every now and then he turned and spoke to the driver of the car in another language. "What language is that you're speaking?" Violet queried.

"It's Hausa, the native language around these parts. Don't worry. You'll be assigned a local guide who'll be able to interpret for you. And it might surprise you, but some of the villagers speak English. It's one of the official languages of Nigeria. You'll get along fine here."

The countryside sped past. They passed some smaller villages, where people were working in the fields, and had to pull over as some livestock were driven along the road toward them.

Violet was feeling nervous.

This was what she'd wanted—a complete change of scenery. A chance to do the job she'd initially set out to do. A chance to test herself again—to get in among real live people and see if she could make a difference to their health and future prospects. A chance to get away from Evan Hunter.

The past few weeks had been a terrible strain. Working with Evan had been hard enough after their passionate interlude. But seeing his reactions to her brother's involvement in the potential smallpox outbreak had made her throw all rational thought out the window.

She'd thought that by applying for a transfer she'd not only get a new start for herself but also a new start away from him.

But the director had obviously had other ideas.

Being trapped in a room with him last night had been more than a little strange. Of course she'd heard him come into the room.

Her heartbeat had quickened as she'd heard the rustle of his clothes. Willing herself not to imagine what lay beneath.

She'd been very conscious of her own breathing, trying not to let it change to keep up the pretense of being asleep when the mattress had sunk as he'd sat down on the edge of the bed. Then there had been the careful placement of pillows between them.

All the while her mind had been throwing them back off the wall on the other side of the room.

But why did she feel like this? She didn't want to like him. She didn't want to find him attractive. It was so much easier when they were arguing and scowling at each other. But this man had crept under her skin in so many different ways that she didn't even want to think about.

All from that one kiss.

Why had neither of them ever acknowledged it? A relationship would have been frowned on by bosses at the DPA. Particularly if things had gone on a downward spiral and affected the work of the team.

But more importantly, for Violet, it was easier to pretend it had never happened. Because then she would have to deal with how it, and he, had made her feel. And she wasn't ready for that, not then and not now.

She wasn't ready for anything other than the job. Thinking about a man would bring a whole host of other emotions to the surface. She was only ready to take baby steps.

Only her first baby steps had been like stepping onto the moon. A giant leap for mankind and a giant leap for Violet.

Working at the DPA had sheltered her for a while. It had almost made her feel safe. Watching the crops and dust speed past was exciting—her first visit to Africa. But it was just so, so different from being based in the DPA at Atlanta.

Could she really handle this? Or was it all just a step too far?

The car jolted to a halt outside a makeshift building. This was obviously the village. Most of it was in a state of disrepair. There was a huge variety of structures from thatched-roof huts to wooden buildings, from brick buildings to some traditionally built *husa* houses.

Her eyes were drawn immediately to the overhead water tank at the edge of the village. At least this village had one. From what she'd learned, access to improved water and sanitation was a daily challenge for most Nigerians, particularly in the rural north of the country where less than half the population had access to safe drinking water and adequate sanitation.

She jumped out and followed Evan into the building. Although the surroundings were poor, the equipment almost made her do a double-take. Two computers sat on a bench—where the generator was she'd no idea. Her eyes widened at the sight of some mobile phones and GPS monitors sitting on another bench, alongside vaccine transporters and fridges into which the vaccines were already being unpacked.

There was whole host of people to meet. Some of the village leaders, some health staff, community outreach workers, midwives and members of another voluntary organization involved in water aid.

But most importantly, outside stood a row of women with their children. Violet cringed with embarrassment as her case thudded from the back of the car. Three months' worth of clothes and a whole pile of other things now seemed extravagant and ridiculous.

It didn't matter that she also had a whole host of medical supplies in her case. The size and weight of her lime-green case now seemed like a beacon of excess. She wanted to send it straight back home.

Evan's much smaller, navy blue case seemed much more appropriate. Something else to hold against him.

Dr. Yusif was still fussing around them, probably relieved that there were finally some colleagues to hand over to. "Your accommodation is over there. I'll get your luggage taken over. Would you like to go and freshen up?"

Violet followed where his finger was pointing at a solid brown building just a few hundred yards away.

"Separate rooms?" she asked. It was the first thing that sprang to mind.

"What?" He looked confused then started laughing. "Of course. There are single rooms for all of our staff. They are small and pretty basic, a single bed with mosquito net, a chest of drawers—" his eyes danced over her bulging case

"—and some toilet facilities, but I'm sure you'll be comfortable."

"I'm sure we will be." She was relieved. Being stuck in a room at night with Evan had unsettled her, and she had no idea if that would be expected in their field assignments too. Thankfully not.

She glanced at her watch, unsure what to do first. She nodded at the people outside. "Want me to get straight to work?"

Dr. Yusif looked a little taken aback. "Don't you and Dr. Hunter want to take some time to settle in? I've got a whole host of things to hand over to Dr. Hunter before I leave—it will probably take the rest of the day."

Violet shrugged. She wasn't there to be a team leader. She was there to be doctor. And there was no time like the present.

Dr. Yusif's hand touched her skin. "You do realize you won't just get to administer polio vaccine straight away? Most of these people are here because their children are sick." He lowered his voice. "This is where it gets really difficult. People come because you're a doctor, not because of the vaccine. If you start to treat every problem, you'll never get the job done that you're here for."

Violet looked at the anxious faces. She could already tell where she would fall down in this job. She couldn't just administer vaccine. She had to look at the whole health of a person, how they lived, their home and their facilities, in order to give them the best advice possible. It was the heart of public health.

"Well, let's just get me started in the meantime. We can reassess how things are going in a few days. Can you pair me up with an interpreter?"

Dr. Yusif nodded quickly and gestured to a young woman dressed in bright clothing to come over. "Olabisi, come over here please."

The woman hurried over, her bright orange and red skirts sweeping along the floor. "Dr. Connelly wants to start straight away. Can you interpret for her, please, and show her around the clinic?"

Evan touched her shoulder. "Are you sure about this?"

He was leaning over her, watching her again with those blue eyes. He was close enough to see the gold flecks.

He couldn't possibly know. He couldn't possibly know how hard these first few steps would be.

Should she tell him?

Of course not. That would be another fault. Another black mark against her name. She'd already kept one secret from him. What would he say if he found out there were two?

He would undoubtedly question her suitability for the job.

But she wanted this. She *needed* this.

Even though it would inevitably break her heart.

It was time to move on.

She turned to face him and met his gaze. "I think it's for the best. If I can get started straight away it will help build some relationships with the villagers."

She could almost hear his brain tick, trying to decide if it was the best thing to do. "I'll come and find you in an hour, okay?"

She nodded and smiled. "That's fine. If there's anyone needing immunization I can do that as I go."

"You're happy with the protocol for recording?"

"It seems straightforward enough. I'll give you a yell if I run into any problems."

He seemed to hesitate, as if he wanted to say

something else, but she didn't wait to find out. She walked to the doorway. Olabisi was already talking to some of the mothers waiting outside, forming them into two separate queues.

"Ah, Dr. Violet." She pointed to the queue on her left. "This one is yours, all these mothers understand English. The other queue is mine. These villagers only speak Hausa. We should be able to get through more this way. Okay?"

Violet smiled. Olabisi was already looking like a professional rather than a local volunteer with rudimentary training. She could learn a lot from these people.

She turned to the first woman in the queue, who was clutching a baby in one arm and holding the hand of another small child with one limb showing clear signs of atrophy. Already they were too late. This child had already been affected by polio.

She gestured with her hand. "Please come in. I'm Dr. Violet."

The afternoon flew past. Polio had blighted this community. Most villagers had probably never even realized they'd been affected. Ninety percent of sufferers had no symptoms.

But then there were the few poor souls—children and adults alike—where the virus had entered their central nervous system and destroyed their motor neurons, leading to muscle weakness and acute flaccid paralysis.

And with the poor sanitation in the village it was no wonder that polio was still spreading.

In the space of a few hours, Violet had delivered and recorded more than forty doses of oral polio vaccine, along with dressing wounds, listening to chests and dealing with a large number of cases of malaria and diarrhea in young children.

But then everything changed.

Then she was faced with a baby.

A really sick baby.

Even before she touched him she could tell instantly how unwell he was.

And she did the worst thing possible. She hesitated.

A horrible sense of dread was sweeping over her. If she could run outside and be sick right now she would. Her mouth felt as dry as a stick as she approached the woman clutching the tiny bundle in her arms.

The words almost stuck in the throat. How awful. How ridiculous. This was exactly why she'd come here. There was no way she could let her nerves get the better of her now.

But this was harder than she'd thought.

This was the first time she'd been in contact with a real, live sick child since her daughter had died.

Her arms trembled as she held them out. "Can I see him, please?"

The mother nodded, burst into tears and handed him over.

Violet held the little bundle in her arms. Aware of the sensations sweeping over her and trying to push them all aside. Trying to keep her "doctor head" in focus. He was seriously underweight, his skin wrinkled with no fatty tissue underneath. According to his mother, after a bout of diarrhea he hadn't been able to eat anything in the last week. It was clear he was severely dehydrated.

Back home a child like this would be rushed into Pediatric Intensive Care, with a central line inserted and IV fluids delivered in a systematic manner to stop overload leading to organ failure. Here, Violet had none of those facilities.

She sat quietly, gently rocking the little boy backward and forward in her arms. Taking a few moments just to gather her thoughts. His eyes were too glazed to focus properly—a clear sign of his ill health.

She spoke quietly to Olabisi. "Do we have any oral rehydration salt sachets?"

Olabisi shook her head. "We go through them so quickly. The Global Children's Support Organization supply us regularly but we're not due another delivery for a couple of days."

Violet nodded. This little boy didn't have a couple of days. He might only have a few hours. She lifted her head. "Could you go and find my case please? Open it up, you'll find some sachets near the back. Bring them to me."

Olabisi bobbed her head and left the room quickly. The sense of dread was leaving Violet. This was a baby who needed comfort. Something else was sweeping over her now.

She felt her lips turn upward and she did the most natural thing in the world to her. Violet started to sing. This little boy needed more than comfort. He needed all the medical care in the world. Children died every day from gastroenteritis and diarrhea, all because of a lack of clean water, sugar and salts. What a difference a little medicine could make. A few sachets could put this little boy on the road to recovery again.

Back in the U.S. some doctors would have given specific instructions to parents to make a suitable solution themselves. But it was a dangerous balance. Too much sugar or salt could upset the child's system. And out here it was wiser to use the ready-prepared solutions.

Violet watched his dark brown eyes while she continued to sing. It would be helpful if there were some antibiotics available too. She'd need to check with Evan if they had their own supplies and could dispense them.

Olabisi gave a shout and the mother stepped outside the room. Violet already knew that Olabisi would be explaining how to use the medicine. The young woman's knowledge and expertise were impressive.

She was left alone with the baby.

For a second it scared her. This was a really

sick little baby. But she was a doctor, she should be used to sick kids.

Only right now she didn't feel like a doctor.

Right now she felt like a mother.

A mother whose heart had been wrenched out.

Her little girl hadn't felt like this. A little bundle of bones.

Her baby had been tiny, well formed and perfect.

Except for the fact she hadn't been breathing.

Violet had been building herself up to this, knowing that at some point she would hold a living, breathing baby in her arms and it would bring back a whole host of bad memories.

But this was different.

And it didn't make her feel the way she'd thought it would.

She didn't want to weep and wail about her own loss. About the lack of rhyme or reason to her perfect daughter being stillborn.

She wanted to weep and wail for *this* baby. For this little boy. For the fact that a few hours of simple medicine could make the difference between life and death for him.

For the fact she *could* do something for this little boy when she hadn't been able to do anything for her own daughter.

And she knew it. She knew it straight away.

She had made the right decision coming here. Evan or no Evan.

Why had she waited so long to do this? Maybe she should have done this straight away, not waited three years until she felt as if her heart had healed.

Maybe if she'd done this sooner she could have moved on with her life, rather than hiding away at a desk job in the DPA.

That first instant, before she'd held him, had been the worst. That had been the moment when she'd thought she would rather do anything else in the world than this. But everyone had experiences like this. The first time doing anything was always the toughest. But always the most worthwhile because it set the scene for what came next.

She cradled the little bundle in her arms. Olabisi arrived a few minutes later with the mother clutching a bottle of the electrolyte mixture, and Violet handed him over with a few extra words.

And then she sat in the fading light in the medical center, watching the mother feeding her child.

Knowing that every weak suck and mouthful gave this child another chance at life.

Grateful that someone had a chance to save their child—even if it wasn't her.

Evan stood in the dying light, watching Violet with the baby in her arms. The handover from Dr. Yusif had taken much longer than expected and he'd gone to the accommodation, expecting to find Violet there.

Instead, he found Olabisi rummaging through Violet's lime-green case for some rehydration sachets. She'd quickly explained what she was doing and he'd followed her back to the clinic, waiting outside while she demonstrated to the mother how to use them.

He was feeling overwhelmed. It wasn't that he felt incapable. He was more than capable of doing this job.

It was just that it was so different from what he'd been used to. He hadn't even really had time to get his head around the fact he was coming to work in Africa for three months before their plane had touched the ground.

This time last week he'd been in the director's office, thinking he was kissing his job and Violet goodbye. This time last week he'd gone to a bar for a drink on the way home, trying to sort out in his head how he could be in Violet's company for the next three months. By the time he'd reached his apartment he had been sure he could keep this entirely professional. It had only taken him a few phone calls to sort out the arrangements for his apartment. No family, no girlfriend to placate, no pets to rehouse. It was kind of sad really, and made him realize how alone he was.

Would anyone miss him while he was gone? His group of male friends had disintegrated in the past few years. Some had moved away as their careers had progressed or splintered in other directions, others had settled down and had families of their own. In the end he'd only had to call a few to let them know he would be gone for a few months and ask them to keep an eye on his place.

So now there was just him and Violet on the outskirts of three local government areas in Nigeria for the next three months.

The "entirely professional" part had worked

until he'd seen her at the airport, with her crumpled white shirt, floral skirt and bare legs. From there on out he'd been fighting a losing battle.

Violet was clearly off-limits. If she'd been interested she would have let him know months ago, after their kiss.

But clearly she wasn't.

And since he was obviously on the director's radar, the last thing he needed was to pay undue attention to another member of staff. Nothing like signing your own death warrant.

So why did watching Violet singing to a sick baby in the dark send a whole host of weird sensations creeping down his spine?

Was it the way she was looking at the baby? The way she seemed to want to soothe it? The gentle way she stroked the side of his face?

Or was it the fact she was so at ease, so comfortable in this strange environment? An environment in which he'd just spent the past few hours wondering how he could keep her safe?

He pressed back against the wall. The heat had dissipated a little now. Would it be cool enough to sleep?

Who was he kidding?

Sleep? With Violet Connelly and her sweet lullabies in the room next door?

Not a chance.

CHAPTER FOUR

"Do you feel up to this?"

The sun had barely risen above the horizon and breakfast was still settling in her stomach at this unearthly hour.

"Of course I am. It's why we're here, isn't it?" She didn't mean to sound tetchy but she couldn't help it.

Evan's eyebrows rose slightly and he handed her one of the GPS transmitters. He sighed. "I still can't believe we can get equipment like this to work out here and some families don't have access to running water. It seems almost absurd."

She nodded. "I know. I'm having trouble making sense of things here. I had another two children at the clinic yesterday affected by polio and their mothers still refused to get their younger siblings immunized. It didn't matter what I said to them."

Evan finished stowing the rest of the vaccines

in the carriers. "They were from the village we're going to this morning?"

Violet nodded. "Olibasi claims most of the children in that village aren't immunized against polio. It's swept through the village twice already. Some of the older adults are virtually paralyzed, but they still won't immunize their children."

His hand came over and rested on her forearm. She tried to ignore the warm sensation that trickled up her arm. "Dr. Yusif left me some notes on that village. They were part of a previous testing trial for another drug for meningitis. Eleven of the children died and many others suffered injuries. Some are blind, some deaf, some kids have brain damage and some liver damage. Is it any wonder the villagers are suspicious? If you were a parent in that village, wouldn't you refuse any other drug offered by strangers?"

Violet felt a tightness spreading across her chest. He'd asked her how she'd feel if she were a parent.

He couldn't possibly know how those words went straight to her heart.

She would have done anything possible to save her child. No matter what that meant. Putting herself into the shoes of these villagers wasn't as difficult for her as Evan might think. Would she have allowed her daughter to be vaccinated by something that might have caused harm?

Absolutely not. Not question about it.

She could almost hear the fear from the villagers. Understand their protectiveness toward their children.

Evan was watching her closely. Waiting to see what her reaction would be.

"I think I would refuse anything that I thought would cause harm to my child." She turned her face away and started searching through her bags, anything to take her away from his close scrutiny. "Here, this is the pictorial flipbook that Olibasi has been using. It's got pictures and health information on health hygiene and sanitation on caring for a baby, as well as information on polio. Gentle persuasion might be the route we have to take, instead of going in with all guns blazing."

Evan smiled at her. The early-morning sun was sending warm orange tones sweeping across the pale earth surrounding them. Why did it make him seem almost…inviting? The midday heat had proved too oppressive for them to work in this last week, so they'd decided to make an early start the norm. But making an early start meant sharing beautiful sunrises with a totally unsuitable man.

Evan had been wrong six months ago and he was still wrong now.

She sucked in a little air. *One step at a time.*

She wasn't ready to consider a relationship of any sort right now—particularly with a man who'd had suspicions about her brother, no matter how good he looked at this time in the morning.

So why did she sometimes feel as if he was sensing the same electricity as she was? The same strange pull?

Was it all in her head? Was the pull just a figment of her imagination? Because in moments like this it felt very real.

His voice cut through her thoughts. "Olibasi is quite an ambassador, isn't she? I'm impressed."

She *was* imagining it. His train of thought was heading in an entirely different direction from hers.

Violet tried to keep the sadness from her tone. "She's fabulous. At another time, in another place she could probably have a whole different career.

It's hard to believe she's only had four years of formal education—it's the same for most women her age. Most of what she's learned has been self-taught."

"Want to secretly train her to be a doctor or a nurse?"

Violet sighed. "I wish I could. I just think of the opportunities I had back home. All because I had a good education. It just seems so unfair that most young girls don't have much formal education." She gestured toward the book. "It's why this works so well. It's difficult to judge someone's level of literacy. And if someone can't read well there's no point in giving them leaflets."

Evan loaded their final supplies into the truck. "From what I've heard, radio is the most popular media in Nigeria. It's ideal for getting the message out to communities, particularly if people are less able to read."

"I've noticed it playing while we've been in the villages. It's like a constant backdrop. Aren't they doing the national campaign for polio via radio?"

He nodded and opened the front door of the truck. "Life expectancy around here is forty-seven years. Thirty percent below the world average. In the U.S. it's seventy-eight. Doesn't it make you feel as if there's a really good reason to be here? To do the work that we're doing?" His eyes looked off into the distance for a second then he jumped up into the truck. "Are you ready? We're picking Olibasi up *en route*."

For a second she was mesmerized by the look on his face. Slowly but surely this man was getting under her skin. It didn't matter what the history was with her brother. It didn't matter that they'd shared a kiss. Evan Hunter was essentially a good man. And it was something that she occasionally forgot in among all her mixed-up feelings about him. Maybe it was time to just focus on that?

He leaned over as she stood at the side of the truck and flicked the switch on her mobile emitter, which was attached to her waistband. The movement was so quick, so unexpected that his warm fingers touching her flesh made her jump.

"Oops, sorry." He pulled his hand back. "We need to keep these switched on. The software has been specially designed to track the daily progress of vaccinators, uploading their routes to the server. It generates maps showing which areas have been covered and highlighting areas of risk."

She slid into the truck next to him, trying to ignore the sensations creeping over her skin. "Like I said, I can't believe that GPS and smartphones work and the water supplies don't."

He started the engine and they set off down the gravel track. "Let's just try and do the best in the situation that we're in. We'll be there in around an hour."

He had his mirrored sunglasses on and a white shirt with the top few buttons unfastened. She could see several light brown hairs curling through the opening.

Nope. It wasn't helping. Even in profile he still looked like a movie star. This was going to be a long day.

The "good man" thoughts were being wiped out in her brain.

Work. She had to focus on work. "How did things go yesterday?"

"It was good. There was a volunteer community mobilizer network targeting caregivers who refused vaccination and children who'd been missed. It was a shame really, lots of kids had missed vaccinations just because they'd been in playgrounds, out in the fields or visiting friends the last time the team was there. They visited eighty households yesterday and immunized one hundred and ninety-three children. Essentially all these children need to be vaccinated four times to be fully protected."

"Wow." Violet leaned back against the burst upholstery. She gave Evan a sidelong smile. "Think we'll match that target today?"

"If only..." His voice sounded wistful. "I've got to just look at the big picture. They tell us if we can get at least one dose of vaccine into the kids who've not been vaccinated, it should give fifty percent of the recipients immunity to the three types of polio. That's got to be worth the trip." He pulled over at the side of the road to let Olibasi join them.

"Violet! You wore the clothes!" She smiled as she jumped in next to them.

Violet shifted in her seat and tugged at the bright pink loose clothing. The longer she was here, the more she realized how unsuitable her normal clothing was. All her white T-shirts were covered in dust, as were her khaki trousers and long skirts. She seemed to trail dust wherever she went. Water was a precious commodity and washing machines weren't exactly available.

Olibasi had arrived with a bag for her the other day containing some more traditional and practical clothing. *Buba* loose-style shirts and *iro* wrap-around skirts. She'd hinted that it might be useful if Violet tried some of the more traditional dress while they were visiting the village today. And even though she wasn't used to the bright colors, already she felt more comfortable.

But the loose clothing still hadn't stopped Evan from touching the bare skin at her waist when he'd flicked the switch on the transmitter. Maybe she should try wearing one of the NASA-style spacesuits they wore in the infectious disease labs at the DPA? It might be the only thing to stop the sensations currently zipping through her skin.

Evan leaned over and switched on the radio. "Relax, ladies. If the road ahead is clear, we'll be there in under an hour."

Evan was trying his best not to stare at Violet's new clothes. Whilst they were much looser than the clothing she normally wore, the vibrant colors suited her and brightened up her skin tone. In a way it was sexier than her usual khaki trousers and white shirt approach—even though it hid the curve of her hips and breasts.

His hands gripped the wheel tighter. *Where had that come from?*

Why was it that every time he thought he'd managed to shoehorn Violet back into the "colleague only" category, his brain liked to throw a wrench into the works? It wasn't as if he didn't have enough work today. He could spend every waking hour planning and organizing their schedules for vaccinations over the next three months.

But every now and then, with one little random glance at Violet, an errant thought would enter his head and he would find that she was first and foremost in his brain.

It was beyond frustrating. Nothing was happening here.

Because Violet seemed oblivious. Sure, sometimes she reacted to his touch but most of the time it didn't seem in a good way.

Most of the time she was totally focused on her work—just like he should be.

Except he couldn't. Not while he was around her.

He still couldn't get over Violet's connection to

Sawyer. And it smarted that she'd kept it quiet. What other secrets was Violet keeping?

The director had been wrong. They weren't learning to work together as a team out here. They were learning to tiptoe around each other as if they were in some skillful dance. Trying to avoid being alone together. Trying to avoid an accidental brush of arms or legs.

Trying to avoid the fleeting eye contact that seemed to stop them both dead and make them oblivious to their surroundings.

So, no, nothing was happening here. Not at all.

Evan focused on the road ahead. Two months, three weeks. That's how much longer he had to last.

No time at all.

"Evan, are you okay in there?"

Violet rattled the wooden door to the make-shift toilet. They'd been working in the villages for hours, but on the way back the truck had got a flat. Evan had changed the bigger-than-average tire, but not before the jack had moved, causing the truck to split the skin on his forearm. "Can I do anything to help you?"

She opened the door just an inch, catching sight of his bare flesh and pulling back just a little. But her curiosity got the better of her. His dust-ridden white shirt lay in a heap on the floor, some blood staining the sleeve.

She edged her head back a little, running her eyes over his wide muscular back. Yup. If he was movie-star material in profile, he was definite movie-star material bare-chested. All defined muscle with not an ounce of fat. It automatically made her suck in her stomach. And made her skin tingle when she realized she'd actually shared a bed with this body.

Was Evan a surfer? Because that's what the defined tone and lines of his body told her. He had a curved scar on his shoulder blade. Flat and well healed. It had obviously been there for years. Where had he got that?

"Seen enough?" The grumpy voice made her jump and she felt her cheeks flush a little at being caught staring.

She straightened her shoulders. "I came to see if I could give you a hand. Do you need stitches? Can I clean your wound for you?" He still hadn't turned around and she was feeling bolder. "Here, let me have a look."

He'd spent the past twenty minutes driving with a blood-soaked rag wrapped around his arm. There was no telling how much dust and grit must be in the wound, and she wanted to inspect it.

There was only a faint trickle of water at the sink. Preservation of water was a must in the village, with their only supply coming from a special tank. Violet screwed up her face when she caught sight of the wound. It was longer and deeper than she'd expected. She caught his wrist in her hands as she leaned forward, trying to ignore the fact his bare chest was only inches away from her. Trying to stop herself from looking.

"I'm sure there's some iodine in the store. I'll go and get some."

He tutted. "Don't fuss, Violet."

She peered at the wound, which was still dotted with little specks of grit. "If I stitch it like this you'll end up with an infection."

"You won't need to stitch it."

"Excuse me?" She lifted her head and raised her eyebrows at him. "I'm the doctor and you're the patient. And just so we're clear—I'll be stitching your wound."

"Oh, it's like that, is it?" There was something different. A different inflection in his voice, a different tone. More humor. A little teasing even.

Her eyes met his.

She and Evan Hunter. Bare-chested in a confined environment. She could see every light brown curly hair on his wide chest. She could see the flecks in his blue eyes again—she was *that* close.

It was tempting. It was *so* tempting.

Her brain spun back to six months before and the feel of his hands on her skin, his lips on her neck. The way that she'd felt that night when she'd finally let go—even if it had just been for a few seconds. She felt herself flush again.

He blinked, but his eyes didn't move. They were still there. Still staring right at her. All she could hear right now was the sound of his breathing. She could see the rise and fall of his chest in her peripheral vision.

But she couldn't pull her eyes away from his.

This really was too close for comfort.

* * *

Something was happening. Something was happening right before his eyes. Violet seemed to stop in her tracks. Her pupils had dilated and her cheeks flushed. The air around them seemed to close in.

She couldn't be thinking the same things that he was, surely? Violet didn't think about him like that, did she? Not since that night when she'd had a few glasses of wine.

What was the story with Violet Connelly?

There didn't seem to be a man in her life. In fact, in the three years she'd been at the DPA he couldn't remember ever hearing Violet refer to a boyfriend or partner.

From his casual enquiries he knew she lived alone.

But why? Why was a knockout like Violet unattached?

She might be prickly around him, but she was warm and gregarious around others. She was well liked. He couldn't imagine she was short of offers, so why didn't she pursue them?

Because right now, in this confined environment, he was looking for an excuse not to act.

In fact, he *needed* an excuse not to act.

It would be so, so easy to lean forward and kiss those plump lips. In fact, he'd been waiting to do it for six months. Six long, long months.

But there had never been a sign, never been even a flicker from Violet. And yet here she was standing in front of him, her pale green eyes almost obliterated by those dilated pupils and her tongue running along her lips. It was enough to drive a man crazy.

Sawyer's sister.

Did he care? Did he really care? His animosity toward Sawyer had burned away at him for years. But Violet affected him in a totally different way. Besides, right now he couldn't think straight. Not when she was biting her lip like that. He took a tiny step forward. His body was starting to react an entirely male way.

She was going to report you for inappropriate behavior. She almost did report you to the director.

What if he was reading this all wrong?

There, that did it.

It stopped him in his tracks. If he kissed her now, what would the consequences be? Would he be accused of seducing her? Of taking advantage of a member of staff? That would be unthinkable.

He stepped back, putting some distance between them.

Violet started. Her eyes widened then she lowered her head.

She *had* expected him to act. She had expected him to kiss her. There was no misreading the confused expression on her face.

"I'll go and get the iodine," she mumbled as she headed out the door.

He shifted uncomfortably. While his body might think he was having a totally normal reaction, his head was telling him differently. Thank goodness she hadn't noticed. It made him feel like some horny teenage boy.

He pulled open the door of the room. Violet and himself in a confined space would have to be avoided at all costs. Not when it caused reactions like this.

She appeared a few seconds later carrying the iodine, some lidocaine and a sterile suturing kit. The flush was gone from her cheeks and her demeanor was entirely professional. "It would probably be best if you sat down while I stitched your arm."

The words sounded a little strained, and definitely formal.

He nodded and sat down at one of the tables while she opened the kit and cleaned his arm, removing all the little pieces of grit before she injected him with some lidocaine to numb the wound. Eleven deftly placed stitches later she placed a non-adhesive dressing over the wound. "Let me know if you have any signs of infection."

She gathered up the waste and disposed of it. "Need anything else?" The question was an entirely innocent one, but it instantly conjured things up in his mind.

This would have to stop, he couldn't continue like this.

She was frozen on her way to the door, looking at him again. Was she thinking about his possible answers to the question?

"Violet? Are you there?"

Their heads turned as one of the other team members appeared in the doorway.

"Yes, I'm here. What is it?"

"There's a call on the satellite phone for you. I think it's your brother."

There. That would do it.

Nothing like slicing the tension in the air with a knife. Nothing like turning the sizzle of electricity into a damp squib.

He could see her bristle. Obviously anticipating his reaction.

She looked a little surprised.

"That's great, thanks. I'll be right there."

Then she walked out the room without a second glance.

CHAPTER FIVE

"WHAT ARE YOU doing in Nigeria, Violet? And when were you planning on telling me?"

Violet sighed and sat down in the nearest seat. This time two weeks ago she would have sold her soul to hear her brother's voice. But right now, when her brain was mush and her body was reacting to things she couldn't seem to control, it really was the last thing she needed.

What had just happened between her and Evan?

"Get off my back. I'd applied for a transfer and the director granted it. We needed to leave at short notice because there were problems in the team. And how was I supposed to get in touch? You were still in the middle of the monkeypox fiasco." She paused, then added, "It's not like keeping in touch has been your priority in the past few years." It was a cheap blow, but she was hoping he'd missed her *faux pas*.

"We? Who is we?" Nope. He'd picked up on it straight away.

She could almost hear the drum roll. "Evan Hunter got transferred too. He's in Nigeria with me." She moved the satellite phone away from her ear. But it didn't matter, the noise reverberated around the room. She'd expected expletives, what she got was deep, hearty laughter.

"Matt? What are you laughing about? Why do you find it funny?"

"I can't believe for a minute he'd request to go to Nigeria! Evan—Mr. Keep-everything-in-order Hunter. He'll hate the chaos out there."

She felt her hackles rise. "He's actually doing okay. The polio program needed a team leader and the director thought Evan might benefit from a change."

"And how would you know this?"

His retort was immediate. And she knew she'd slipped up. There was no way she should know that—no way she should have heard the director telling Evan that. She tried to turn the conversation around. "How did you find out I was here, anyway?"

"The director. He's been speaking to me every

day. Trying to persuade me that there is a role for me at the DPA. But I'm still undecided."

"Really?" It was first good news she'd heard. Sawyer had been so set against the DPA when his wife had died. But the past few weeks' experience had obviously changed his perspective. Things must be changing for him. She smiled. "Is someone helping you make this decision? A certain blonde someone?"

"Sis…" He sighed. "Give it up."

"What's happening with you and Callie? Are you seeing her? Remember, I warned you. I like Callie a lot." She felt her stomach clench a little. Her brother had been distraught when his wife had died on a mission with him and Evan. After six years, meeting Callie had finally put a little joy into his voice again. She really didn't want him to screw this up.

"Callie is good. No, scratch that. Callie is *great*." She could almost see the grin on his face, "We're going to take things slowly, but I like that. I like *her*."

"Should I buy my wedding hat?"

He hesitated and her heart leaped. *Matt, really, thinking about that again?* "I'm taking it slowly—remember? But maybe you'll need one in the future." He changed the subject quickly. "How are you getting on with Evan? Is he treating you okay?"

How did she answer that? That he was keeping her mind from the job and could potentially lead her astray? That she felt as if her skin was on fire every time he brushed against her? That she could have almost put money on the fact he'd been about to kiss her and then he'd stopped? That she didn't feel ready for any of this?

"He's a good team leader," she said quietly.

"What? Tell me you didn't just say that?"

She straightened in her chair. What did he mean? Did he still hold a grudge because Evan had been team leader when his wife had died? Was there always going to be this animosity between them?

"Listen, Sawyer, I know you probably don't rate him. And I wasn't there all those years ago, so I don't know what happened between you. But Evan seems to be a good team leader. He's diligent. He's professional. He's organized."

"Whoa, sis, stop right there. You sound like you're giving me a reference for a business partner, not telling me how the person you've traveled with to the other side of the world is treating you."

"Oh." She pressed her lips together to stop herself from putting her foot in it any further.

But Sawyer hadn't finished. "I know we've never spoken about this, but I want to make sure he's treating you okay. Evan and I—there isn't a lot of love lost between us. My wife died—I was upset. My behavior could have been better. A lot has gone down between us in the past and none of it has ever really been resolved. I'm not sure what his take is on everything, but I don't really care. What I care about is my sister. Are you okay, sis?"

She held her tongue. How long had she waited to hear those words? What wouldn't she have given to hear those words three years ago, when she'd felt all alone in the world with a baby to bury?

She blinked back the tears. Thank goodness Sawyer wasn't here, looking into her eyes. He would know straight away that she was hiding something. And she couldn't have that conversation with him yet. Maybe never.

Things had been so bad back then. Her mom and stepdad and been devastated when Matt's wife had died from an ectopic pregnancy. Their daughter-in-law and potential grandchild wiped out in one fell swoop. Not to mention a son who had then shut himself off from the world and disappeared. They hadn't coped. They hadn't coped at all.

So when she herself had fallen pregnant unexpectedly, she had felt as if she couldn't tell them. They would have worried themselves sick. Particularly when they found out she'd chosen to go it alone. Her relationship with Blane had been serious but they had both been so focused on their careers, his in business and hers in medicine, that a baby had never been part of that equation. It had been no surprise when he'd walked away.

So she'd decided to wait. To wait until she had a brand-new granddaughter to present to them. They might be a little shocked, but the arrival of a new grandchild would overcome all of that.

They would have been delighted.

If only it had all worked out that way.

Instead, she'd been left alone with only a few close friends for comfort. She couldn't tell them—no matter how much she needed them. It would have broken their hearts all over again. They were frail enough as it was.

And now she was here. Three years on. Trying to move on with her life.

First steps. She was still taking the first steps. "I'm fine, Sawyer. I'll keep in touch, okay?" There was so much they probably had to say to each other, but now just wasn't the time. She hung up the phone quickly before he had a chance to say anything else.

It only took her a few moments to get outside. Tears were threatening to spill down her cheeks. She had to get a hold of herself. It was time to move on.

Across on the other side of the village she could see a small gathering of people. Maybe some new arrivals? There seemed to be a few new families in the village every day. She picked up one of the flipbooks about the vaccine.

It was time to get back to work. And there was no time like the present.

"Evan, can you come and look at a child for me, please?"

He pulled himself away from the computer-generated program that was running, plotting where they still needed to vaccinate.

"Sure. What's up?" He stood up from the chair and cricked his back. He'd been sitting too long and was getting stiff. It was time to do some leg work.

"One of the children we vaccinated yesterday isn't looking too well. Can you come and see him?"

He nodded and grabbed his stethoscope and small bag. The mother was in one of the rooms with Olibasi, the small child clutched in her arms. Tears were streaming down her face and she was talking frantically.

Evan walked over quickly and held his hands out for the baby. "What's wrong, Olibasi?"

Olibasi hesitated, her face serious. "This is Nkoyo. I'll need to translate as she doesn't speak any English. She says her son has become unwell since receiving his first vaccine yesterday. She thinks it's given him polio."

Evan raised his head quickly. "How old is her son?"

The little boy in his lap was obviously underweight and underdeveloped. Vaccine-associated paralytic polio was rare, but the risk in immuno-deficient children was around seven thousand times higher. A major concern about the oral polio vaccine was its known ability to revert to a form that could cause neurological infection and paralysis—but not this quickly.

"He's one year."

Evan took in a sharp breath. The baby looked around seven months and didn't appear to be meeting his developmental milestones. He couldn't sit or grasp with his hands. His temperature was low and his abdomen distended. His skin was dry and peeling and his hair thin and discolored. His arms and legs were extremely thin. His head was rolling from side to side and he was limp in Evan's arms.

He quickly sounded the child's chest. "Check with his mum—he was okay yesterday? He didn't feel cold? His belly wasn't distended like this?"

His brain was working frantically. Whatever was wrong with this child was serious. Olibasi was talking in a low voice to the mother. She was shaking her head.

"I think he's been unwell for a longer than a day. His abdomen has been distended for a while and he's had chronic diarrhea. He hasn't been eating."

Evan took a deep breath. "Has his mother stopped breastfeeding him recently?"

Olibasi turned back to the mother. "Yes, she has. The family don't have much food. She says she wasn't producing enough milk."

"Who gave the baby the vaccine?"

"One of the community mobilizers."

"And they're not from this village? Have you ever seen this baby before?"

Olibasi shook her head. "They're from an out-lying village. This is the first time they've come here."

Evan ran his finger over the child's skin again. He was sure he knew what was wrong. But how he explained it to the mother would be most important. The last thing he wanted to do was make her feel responsible.

He cleared his throat. "Tell her it's definitely not the vaccine. It couldn't cause effects like this so quickly. Vaccine-associated paralytic polio is very rare—about one case per seven hundred and fifty thousand vaccine recipients. And it's more likely to occur in adults than in children."

Olibasi took a few moments to translate to the mother. "She wants to know what's wrong with her son."

Evan gave her his best reassuring smile and tried to tread carefully. "I think her son is suffering from a type of protein-energy malnutrition called kwashiorkor. It develops in babies who've been weaned from breast milk and who often suffer from other conditions like chronic diarrhea. It causes stunted growth and wasting of muscle and tissue." He reached over and put his hand on Olibasi's arm. "Be careful how you translate. This condition hasn't appeared overnight. Do you think the vaccine gave her an excuse to bring her baby to the village?"

Olibasi's eyes darkened and she gave just the slightest nod of her head. "Give me a few moments to speak with her."

Evan kept the little boy in his arms and went to the supply closet. This was the first real case of malnutrition he'd seen since he'd got here. And it was heartbreaking. Back home this child would have bloods taken and be admitted to hospital and given intravenous fluids or tube-fed if required. But out here the options were distinctly limited.

He found some first-line electrolyte solutions and some supplements. It felt inadequate but was the best he could do. "Ask her if she's willing to stay in the village for a few days. Tell her it's really important." There was a real chance that the little boy would be left with an inability to absorb nutrients properly through his intestines, so it was essential that they monitor him in some way.

Olibasi took the sachets from his hands. "I'll do my best to persuade her. I'm sure I can find somewhere for them to sleep. Do you want to see him again?"

Evan nodded. "Every day for the next few days. We need to see if he starts to improve." He handed the little boy back to his mother.

Olibasi slid her arm around the woman's shoulder and led her outside. Evan picked up a file and started to scribble some notes. It didn't matter that they were there to administer the polio vaccine. It didn't matter that they really shouldn't get involved in all the general medical problems of the villagers.

What mattered most was building rapport with

these people. Building an element of trust. There was enough miscommunication about the polio vaccine already. How else could a woman in an outlying village know about vaccine-associated polio paralysis?

It was the age-old problem. Nothing spread quicker than a bad news story.

If word had got out that the polio vaccination had caused that child's illness it would be a disaster. It didn't matter that it had nothing to do with it. It was what the villagers believed that mattered. And Evan could only do his best to try and contain the situation and get the little boy on the road to recovery.

"You did good."

He jumped. Violet was standing in the doorway, her figure silhouetted against the ebbing sun.

He stood up and walked over to her. "You were listening?"

She gave him a little smile. "I was coming to see you. When I saw you were consulting with a patient I decided to wait. It was nice getting to see you play doctor."

He folded his arms and leaned against the doorjamb. "Play doctor. That's what it feels like." His eyes fixed out on the setting sun in front of them. "I understand why we're here—I really do. And I understand the rationale about not getting caught up in other issues. Not to lose sight of our task." He flung up his hands in exasperation.

"But how can we realistically do that? The polio work has to come hand in hand with the welfare of these people. I can't ignore malnutrition—even if I don't have the right tools to prevent it. I can't ignore malaria—even if I have to beg another agency for mosquito nets. And I can't ignore the sanitation problems. Because they are connected to everything else." He shook his head. "But I feel like there will never be enough supplies or equipment to do the job we really need to do."

He looked down at Violet. She was watching him carefully and he knew instantly that she understood. She understood his frustration about all the things that were outside their control. She understood that he was going to spend the rest of the night worrying about that little boy and whether he would make it through till morning.

And he didn't need to say any more. Because Violet just moved. And it happened naturally.

She shifted her feet and leaned against him, making it seem like the most natural thing in the world to rest his arm around her shoulder.

She rested her head against his chest. Could she hear the beating of his heart?

Her voice was quiet. "The things we can't control will always be the hardest. Particularly when we can't even understand some of them."

There was something else. Something he hadn't heard before.

For the first time he felt as if he'd picked away at one of Violet's unending layers. She wasn't just talking about here and their situation. Yes, it was part of it, but she was also talking about something else.

It was so calm, so peaceful right now. And he didn't want to destroy this. He didn't want to destroy this moment. It would be so easy to ask her if something was bothering her. It would be so easy to pry. But he didn't want to take a chisel and chip away at her layers. He didn't want to back her into a corner. He had to let her unpeel her layers herself.

Maybe he'd never reach the center of Violet Connelly. But it might be nice to wait around and see.

He chose his words carefully. "Maybe we're not meant to understand everything, Violet. Maybe we're not here to change the world. Maybe we're just meant to learn how to live through it."

She gave a quiet murmur and lifted her hand and placed it on his chest.

And the two of them stood, watching the sun set over the wide landscape in front of them.

CHAPTER SIX

THE MEETING ROOM was crowded. Evan's meticulous planning for the polio campaign was going well. The huge map on the wall and the corresponding graph with the number of vaccines delivered was impressive by anybody's standards.

But it wasn't good enough for Evan. And Violet wasn't surprised.

He clapped his hands together to draw the chattering crowd to attention. "Thanks for coming, everyone. I wanted to look at a few ways we can improve the total uptake of the polio vaccine and give added protection to the people of Natumba."

He pointed to a certain area on the map on the wall. "There are a few villages where there is a high rate of refusal." He nodded to one of the community volunteers. "I've arranged a series of meetings between the volunteers, ourselves and some of the village elders. We need to work in partnership with these people if we want to make any lasting improvements."

Violet heard the mutterings around her. Lots of attempts had been made in the past to try and increase the uptake of polio in these villages but Evan's persistence might pay off. He'd spent time in these villages in the past few weeks, taking time to get to know the elders and some of the health issues facing the inhabitants. He was slowly but surely gaining their trust and that had to help.

He pointed to another area on the map. "We still haven't made much headway mapping the Fulani nomadic routes. Most of the Fulani people haven't been vaccinated and they have a high rate of individuals affected by polio. It's always difficult to try and target a group of people who are constantly on the move. But we've had some news that they are about to arrive in our local area and we want to be ready."

He nodded to one of the Healthy World Federation members of staff in the room. "Dr. Brasi will be leading the team this week that will be attempting to make contact with the Fulani people and vaccinate them."

Violet smiled. It all made sense. Evan was being methodical and consistent in his approaches. The number of people vaccinated was rising every day. Surely they would meet the targets they had been given?

"And finally..." He paused, his eyes meeting Violet's for a second. She felt her heart flutter a little. They hadn't been alone together since that night when they'd watched the sunset. Once the sky had darkened he'd given her hand a little squeeze and walked her to her room.

Her heart had sunk a little when she'd realized he wasn't going to attempt to kiss her. Then she'd lain awake wondering why she wanted him to kiss her. Nothing made sense to her anymore. Her head kept telling her she wasn't ready for any of that kind of thing, but her body was reacting differently.

He gave her a little smile. "One of the areas we need to improve on is new births. Newborns need to be tracked and immunized through the midwife service scheme, with oral polio vaccine being placed in delivery rooms to ensure administration of a dose at birth. We need to strengthen links with traditional birth attendants and traditional leaders." He paused for a moment. "And I'm going to ask Dr. Connelly to lead on this."

What?

Her smile froze in place. Why hadn't he talked to her about this beforehand? He gave her a little nod and continued talking, totally unaware of what he'd just unleashed.

Violet couldn't move. Her brain was mush. Her heartbeat was quickening in her chest—and not in a good way. She felt sick.

He had no idea. He had no idea at all at what he was asking of her.

But, then, how could he? Because she hadn't told him what had happened to her. He couldn't possibly know that the last time she'd been in a delivery room had been the worst day of her life.

The day she had welcomed her daughter into the world and then bid her farewell.

How on earth could she cope with being in that environment every day?

She took a deep breath.

She was a doctor. This was her job. She had wanted to come here—she wanted to move on.

It had been three years, and a birthing room here would be nothing like a delivery room back home. How could it evoke the same memories and experiences?

All she was being asked to do was set up links with local midwives and birth attendants. She wasn't being asked to *be* in the delivery rooms.

But that thought didn't stop her thudding heart. She wasn't stupid. She'd done her research before she'd arrived in Nigeria.

The stillbirth rate in Nigeria was one of the highest in the world, with half occurring while the woman was in labor. It was inevitable that she would come across one at some point in the three months that she was here.

Evan was still talking. And people were listening. He was captivating his audience with his enthusiasm and passion for the tasks ahead. Heads were nodding all around them and people were shouting out suggestions and ideas.

Would she be able to face the challenges ahead with the same enthusiasm and passion?

Her eyes fixed on her hands. It was easier than looking at Evan. Most of her nails were broken and her skin was starting to tan lightly in spite of the sunblock she was constantly applying. Back home she'd had her nails manicured every month. But the truth was she didn't even miss it.

While the lifestyle out here was tough—no hot running showers, no wide array of facilities, no hair salons, no easy transport—the experience she was gaining was far outweighing the negatives. Even working with Evan wasn't as bad as she'd feared.

Why had she wanted to get away from him so badly? Was it really because of the issues with her brother? Or was it the fact that she didn't want to face up to how she felt about him?

Whatever it was, she didn't have brain space for it right now. Getting through the work with the midwives would be a tough enough challenge.

And one that would take up all her emotional energy and spirit.

He'd noticed it. Even though she didn't realize.

But, then, he noticed everything about her.

That fleeting moment, that wave of fear that had seemed to pass over her eyes.

What did it mean? Or had he just imagined it?

He couldn't trust anything he felt around Violet Connelly. His instincts seemed to be completely wrong around her. She messed with his mind. Ten minutes in Violet's company and all rational thought went out the window.

He'd thought she'd be happy that he'd assigned her a specific task she could get her teeth into. Something she could lead and tackle on her own. Giving her the midwifery role had seemed to make sense.

He'd been watching her. She was wonderful around babies and children. She seemed to come into her own. She excelled at dealing with them. This job should have been perfect for her.

So why the fear in her eyes?

But something else was bothering him. Something else was eating at his stomach.

Was that really the reason he'd given her this task?

Or had he just wanted to avoid it himself?

Evan had no reason to avoid children or babies. But he did have a reason to avoid pregnant women.

Helen. Sawyer's wife.

She'd died of an ectopic pregnancy. No one had known she was pregnant. Not Sawyer, and apparently not Helen.

And seeing pregnant women immediately brought Helen to mind.

It hadn't been as though she'd looked pregnant—not as if a glance at a pregnant woman reminded him directly of Helen.

No, it just reminded him of what *should* have been Helen.

And that's what made him sick to his stomach.

He'd spent the past few years thinking that Sawyer must have known his wife was pregnant. They both must have known and kept it secret, otherwise Helen would never have been allowed to go on the mission in the first place.

But that was an excuse. And it was a poor excuse.

It was so easy to push the blame onto Sawyer and not to take any responsibility himself. But he had been the team leader. He had been the one responsible for the health and wellbeing of everyone in his team. And Helen had told him she wasn't feeling one hundred percent.

It had been a fleeting comment. An unremarkable conversation. And if Evan hadn't been so caught up in the details of the mission he might have stopped for a minute to consider what she'd said.

He could have asked her a few questions about what was wrong, and to specify exactly how she was feeling. And he knew, deep down, that at some point there was a tiny chance he might have asked her if there was a possibility she was pregnant.

And even though Helen hadn't known herself, it might have given her pause to stop and think and consider the possibility. It might have made her stop for a second and do a pregnancy test.

Bottom line. It might have saved her life.

The ectopic pregnancy had been a horrible inevitability for Helen. But where it occurred wasn't.

If she'd been in Atlanta when she'd had the symptoms, she would have gone to the nearest hospital and undergone surgery. And lived.

But none of that had happened. And the sight of Helen lying in her husband's arms, with the life slowing but surely seeping out of her, had haunted Evan for the past six years.

He had been the team leader. Helen had been his responsibility.

He'd never shared this with anyone. And he

never would. Least of all with a member of Sawyer's family.

He watched as the team assembled around him, Violet among them, talking quietly with some of the voluntary workers.

Another team he was responsible for. Another team whose lives were in his hands.

He could do this. He could. He just had to focus and keep his mind on the job.

He had to keep his eyes and ears open to the health and wellbeing of his team. Which meant he had to get to the bottom of what was wrong with Violet. She was his responsibility—whether she liked it or not. And he couldn't ignore the fact that something could be going on with her. He wouldn't be able to live with himself if he missed something in a team member again.

He watched for a few seconds. Violet was fidgeting with her flower-covered notebook, picking away at the edges as she spoke to someone. Every few moments she would bite her lip. She put her notebook down and her fingers went automatically first to her ear then to a strand of hair that she wound round and round one of her fingers.

The person she was talking to seemed oblivious to Violet's nerves. They were talking quickly, gesturing with their hands, only taking notice of her occasional nods.

Was that how he'd been with Helen? So wrapped up in other things that he hadn't looked at what had been right in front of him, or listened to her words?

It made him feel sick to his stomach.

Violet looked over and for a second those pale green eyes met his. Every muscle in his body tightened but she instantly averted her gaze, reluctant to let him read anything at all.

It only made him more determined.

He couldn't decide if he'd given her the midwifery role because he wanted to avoid it himself or whether he'd given it to her to show how much he valued her as a part of the team. But that was irrelevant.

What was important was what happened next. What *he* did next.

And that was the one thing that he could control.

CHAPTER SEVEN

EVAN WAS IN a good place. They'd immunized over one hundred people today, the majority of them children.

It was a good outcome for the team, giving them the boost that they'd needed. The past few days had been tough on them. Several visits to villages had been unproductive, with hours spent going from house to house, even though most people were still refusing to be vaccinated. It was heartbreaking. All around them there were signs of the destructiveness of polio and its lasting effects. Some elderly villagers, struggling for every breath, their chest muscles virtually paralyzed by polio. The first sign of an infection would wipe them out.

Children of various ages with one weak, wasted limb affecting their mobility—and parents still wouldn't immunize their other children.

It didn't help that the one thing he'd dreaded

had finally happened. One of the few families that had been vaccinated had actually given vaccine-associated paralytic polio to one of their distant adult cousins. It was a rare complication, usually caused by an adult changing the nappy of a recently vaccinated child and picking up the disease due to poor hand washing. But it was a blow the team didn't need.

Evan felt as if he were banging his head on a brick wall. Things had to be better than this.

And now they were here. This village had welcomed them with open arms. People had queued for hours to be vaccinated, bringing family members of all ages. And the community workers had come back with a list of houses to visit where people were unable to come to the clinic but still wanted to be vaccinated.

It didn't matter that it was more time-consuming and difficult. Evan didn't care. He would happily walk around every home in the village individually if that's what it took to get everyone vaccinated.

Time was marching on. It had been a long day—they'd been here nearly ten hours and they still had an hour's drive back home.

He approached one of the final houses, a lightweight structure made of a mixture of wood, bricks and mud. Jaja, his community worker, gave him a smile as they approached the house. "This lady has four children she wants vaccinated. She would have come to the clinic but one of her sons, Dumkata, has been very sick these past few days."

Jaja pushed opened the door to the house and engaged in a long conversation with the mother, who seemed more than happy to see them.

But Evan's eyes were drawn to the corner of the room, where a small boy was lying on a makeshift bed. His siblings were playing around him and he seemed oblivious to the noise in the room. Evan's instincts were automatic and he went to the bed of the sickly child.

"Hi, there, Dumkata."

The dark eyes flickered open at the sound of the foreign voice. The little boy's hands automatically started scratching at his skin, as if he had an uncontrollable itch. It was almost as if Evan's voice had broken him out of the half-slumber he'd been in.

Evan turned to face Jaja. "Can you ask the mother if she minds if I take a look at her son?"

Jaja answered quickly. "She was just asking me the same thing. She knows you're only here to give the vaccinations and didn't want to take up your time."

"It's no problem. I'm happy to look at him. Can you organize the polio vaccination for the rest of the family, Jaja?"

The community worker nodded and pulled out the vaccine carrier and flip book to explain things to the family.

Evan touched Dumkata's forehead. It was just as he'd expected. Burning hot. He pulled his medical bag over and took out the tympanic thermometer. It beeped within a few seconds. It indicated that the boy had a temperature.

He pulled out his stethoscope to sound the little boy's chest. Dumkata barely responded, he still seemed fixated on the itch in his skin. "Can you ask the mother what he's been complaining of?"

Jaja took a few moments to reply. "She says he's had a terrible headache for the past few days and his joints are painful and sore. Dumkata is usually running about constantly. She says this is not like him."

Evan nodded and gestured to Jaja. "Could you help me sit him up for a moment, please?"

Something was setting off alarm bells in Evan's head. He had the strangest feeling, and experience told him to go with his instincts.

He spent some time examining Dumkata's skin. There were a few angry marks—just like bee stings—along with a rash that was difficult to see on Dumkata's dark skin and some swelling in the subcutaneous tissues.

He pressed his fingers gently around Dumkata's neck and groin, checking the lymph glands and finding them enlarged. It was clear that some type of infection was circulating around the child's body.

"Can you go and find Violet for me, please? I'd like to have a chat with her."

Jaja nodded and slipped out of the door. Violet had been working in the village today too but their paths had barely crossed. They'd mapped out the village and decided on separate routes to try and cover the majority of people who had requested to be seen. It made more sense for them to split up than work together.

It also prevented any awkward conversations or, more likely, awkward silences.

It was almost as if she was deliberately avoiding him. She'd never complained about working with the midwives and birth attendants. She'd just put her head down and got on with the job.

But he hadn't forgotten the look in her eyes. Or the way she'd realized that he'd noticed. At some point they were going to have to have that conversation. If he'd learned anything these past few years it was he needed to be sure about the welfare of his team.

The little form moved on the bed in front of him. He tried to focus on the matter at hand. The niggling feeling he had in his gut about this little boy.

Violet appeared in the doorway. "Evan? You were looking for me?"

Pretty as a picture—even after ten hours on the job. She was wearing another of Olibasi's outfits, this time in pale pink instead of the brighter colours. Her blond hair was swept up in a clip and her normally pale skin was starting to tan slightly.

Olibasi had been right about the effect of wearing local clothes. Violet seemed to be widely accepted wherever they went. Some reports on previous villages had been a little alarming. But in the past few weeks Violet seemed to be getting good results. The uptake of the polio vaccine was rising in places where it had previously stalled.

It didn't make sense that it was all down to the type of clothes that the doctor wore. Violet's quiet, easy nature and never-ending patience was obviously a major factor. But the fact she wore the clothes so well wouldn't exactly be a hindrance. He tried to keep the smile from his face.

"Thanks, Violet. I know we're just about to finish up but I wondered if you'd mind brainstorming with me for a minute."

She looked a little surprised but took it in her stride. "No problem." She crossed the room and kneeled down next to him at the side of the bed. "Who do we have here?"

"This is Dumkata—he's seven. According to his mom he's usually the life and soul of the party, but he's been unwell these past few days.

He has a temperature, a headache, sore joints with some noticeable swelling, some bites and swollen lymph glands." He caught Dumkata's hand as it started to scratch again. "He also seems to have an irritating itch."

Violet nodded. "Well, it could be whole host of things with those symptoms. What's worrying you most?"

Evan scratched his chin. "Probably the bites." He turned to face her. "Probably my gut instinct." He shook his head. "I'm just not happy."

She nodded. "Then let's be methodical about this. Is anything springing to mind?"

She bent over Dumkata and started examining his skin. The rash was difficult to determine but was widespread across his skin. It appeared mainly to be speading out from the two bite marks on his skin. "Does the mom know what caused these bites? Is there something in particular we should be considering?"

Evan wrinkled his nose. "Probably. It's frustrating. Back home we've got everything to hand. Out here it's much more difficult."

Violet gave him a little smile. She understood completely. Back at the DPA they had a computer program for everything. Every tiny sign or symptom all calculated and computed to tell you any possibilities and what to look for next. She pulled a tiny pocketbook from under her traditional skirt. "Want a look at this?"

It was a copy of a tropical disease handbook—ten years old and obviously well worn. She'd had it since she'd been a student and had hardly looked at it in recent years. But it had been a last-minute addition to her suitcase.

As Evan turned the pages, one fell out in his hands. "Sorry," she muttered. "I'm sure I've got some sticky tape somewhere."

Jaja walked over to them. "The mother has no idea what the bites are. Her son was playing out near the fields a few days ago. He came home with the bites. She hasn't seen them before and Dumkata just said they were bee stings."

Evan's head shot up. It was almost as if a little light had just gone on in his head. He started muttering and flicking through Violet's book, "Fields...flies..." His eyes met hers.

"What about tsetse flies? What about the first signs of sleeping sickness?"

"Really? I thought that had almost disappeared?"

Evan pulled out his PDA and looked up some files. He frowned. "Only two cases reported in Nigeria last year. Could it really be something like that?"

Violet shook her head. "You'll have to remind me about it. I can't remember that much."

His eyes scanned between the screen and the book he held in his hands. "African trypanosomiasis is a vector-borne parasitic disease, known as sleeping sickness. The parasites are transmitted to humans by the bite of the tsetse fly. Most common in areas of fishing, animal husbandry or—" he lifted his eyes to meet hers "—agriculture."

"What do the flies look like?"

He shook his head. "There aren't any pictures. It just says they are about the same size as bees and quite aggressive."

Violet looked over at the mother. Jaja was doing his best to relay their conversation to her and the distress on her face was visible. She rushed over and put her arm around her child.

"Help my baby."

Violet could feel her stomach muscles clench at her reaction. The instant fear that something could happen to her child—something completely out of her control.

She took a slow breath. "We need to stay focused. Does it list the signs and symptoms?" She lowered her voice slightly. "How serious is it? Do we have anything to treat it?"

Evan's eyes were still flickering back and forth between the book and the screen. "The signs and symptoms are compatible with the first stage. The temperature, itching, joint pains and headaches. They are all signs that the trypanosomes are multiplying in the subcutaneous tissues. It's called the haemolymphatic phase."

Violet could almost feel her own skin start to itch at the thought of parasites circulating around the little boy's body. It was horrible.

She tried to pull her doctor's head back into focus. She was finding it so hard not to look at Dumkata's mother and see the pain and fear in her eyes. Even though this was an entirely different situation from her own she wanted to reach out and tell her that she understood. That she knew the fear of the unknown, the protectiveness she was feeling and the helplessness at things being out of her control.

"How do we diagnose this?"

"We need to take a blood test. It used to be really difficult to diagnose because the number of parasites in the blood can be low and they need to be separated from the red blood cells." He pointed to something on the screen. "There's a pan-African campaign on the eradication of try-panosomosis. Let me see if can get some more details." He pulled out his satellite phone and pressed in a number as he headed toward the doorway. "Give me a few minutes."

Violet nodded as she watched him leave. "Jaja, can you come and sit with us? I'd like you to translate for me, please."

Violet's eyes flickered over the screen as she picked up some more details. She finally had the courage to meet Dumkata's mother's eyes. "Tell her we need to make a diagnosis and Dr. Hunter is just finding out the best way to do that." She watched as Jaja rapidly translated. "Tell her we think that if it is sleeping sickness, then it's been caught at an early stage—a stage that can be treated."

Within a few seconds she could see the relief as the woman relaxed her shoulders and shot some rapid questions at Jaja. He gave her a few answers, obviously trying to reassure her, then turned back to Violet. "She wants to know how long it takes and what the treatment is."

Violet nodded. It's the kind of thing she'd want to know too. Evan appeared back in the doorway. He gave her a wide smile—obviously good news. His broad shoulders filled the door way and the tired look that had haunted him for the past few days had disappeared.

The African sun was agreeing with him. His skin had already been a light golden-brown that was deepening with every day. It only succeeded in making his teeth look whiter than ever and his blue eyes more prominent. His brown hair was lightening in the sun, giving the ends blond tips. She couldn't have achieved that look even if she'd spent ten hours in the hair salon. Her hair was becoming more brittle day by day. The leave-in conditioner she was using every other day in an attempt to waylay the damage made her hair feel slimy. Hardly a good look, by anybody's standards. Why did men have things so much easier?

She was still struggling with the task he'd given her last week. Not that she wanted anyone to know that.

By anyone else's standards she was doing fine. She'd reached out to the midwives in the neighboring villages and arranged to spend time with them all.

But a few had made it clear she'd need to see them on their own terms. Which was likely to mean in the middle of someone's home or the local birthing room.

All things that made her bristle with nerves and wonder if she could manage this.

Having Evan here today had been a welcome break from her other work. Even though they hadn't been working side by side today it was almost a comfort to have him around. To know that another doctor had her back in case they got into any difficulties.

It gave her even more of a buzz to know that he'd wanted her opinion—had valued her opinion on a case. He had confidence in her abilities, even if she sometimes doubted them.

Evan crossed the room toward them. "The news is good. All I need to do today is take a blood sample. It used to be difficult to separate the parasites from the blood cells but we're in luck. Some Swedish scientists have developed a microfluidic device that separates the parasites from the blood cells using their shape, because parasites and red blood cells are very difficult to separate by size. It's being trialed in one of the local labs and they're going to arrange to pick up our sample." He placed his hand on Dumkata's mother's shoulders. "We should have the results very soon."

Jaja was speaking quickly, translating everything that Evan had said. She asked another question and he turned back to Evan. "And the treatment?"

Evan nodded. "We'll need to do one other test if the blood test is positive—a lumbar puncture. Tell her we'll take a little sample of Dumkata's spinal fluid. It gives a clear indication of what stage the disease is at. We suspect it's in the first stage and if that's confirmed, the treatment is relatively simple, a drug—pentamidine, which is supplied free of charge by the Healthy World Federation."

He waited a few minutes for Jaja to relay the

news. Dumkata's mother seemed satisfied with the answers but Violet stood up in front of him.

"It all seems too good to be true. What happens if the disease is further on than we expect?"

Evan frowned and lowered his voice. "I'm pretty sure it's not. We're lucky they are trialing the new diagnosis system here. It should give a much more accurate result."

Violet raised her eyebrow. He still hadn't really answered her question, and it was the second time she'd asked. It was as if he were playing a careful game of dodgeball with her. She looked over her shoulder. Dumkata's mother couldn't hear them speak right now.

"I can't remember, but is sleeping sickness fatal if it's not diagnosed early enough?"

His eyes fixed on hers and he gave a little sigh. "Well, yes, it can be. The second stage isn't too pleasant. The parasites cross the blood-brain barrier and infect the central nervous system. It causes neurological damage, bringing confusion, sensory disturbances, poor co-ordination and disturbance of the sleep cycle—it's what gave the disease its name." His eyes drifted over to the other side of the room to the little figure huddled up in the bedclothes. "At that stage, it can be fatal."

She reached over and touched his arm, trying to ignore the way the hairs on her own arm reacted. "But we're not at that stage, are we?" She gave his arm a little tug to move outside. "How do you feel about doing the lumbar puncture? Are you happy to do it? I can do it if you want. I have to put my hands up and admit it's been a little while since I've done one."

He shook his head, his eyes fixed on the fact she still had her hand on his arm. She hadn't really wanted to move it but the intensity of his gaze made her pull her hand away.

"No, it's fine, Violet. I cover on a regular basis on a pediatric unit. I'm happy to do the lumbar puncture."

She tried not to let the sense of relief she felt show. "You do? Why have you never mentioned it?"

He sighed, his eyes on her face. "We don't exactly have these social conversations, do we?"

She felt her face flush. He wasn't saying the words but he didn't have to. She was always quick to rebuff any of Evan's attempts at small talk. It was her own small measure of self-protection. The less she knew about him, the less she could feel.

But she was moving on. She was attempting to feel in control again.

He was still staring at her and she felt very self-conscious under his gaze. She couldn't imagine how she looked after ten hours in the claustrophobic heat. She probably looked like the equivalent of a well-cooked sausage. Hardly an attractive prospect.

But the timing felt right. The way Evan was looking at her was speaking volumes to her. She glanced over her shoulder. And it was just them. No one else was around.

She took a step forward. It was tiny—literally just a few inches. But it felt like jumping off the edge of a cliff.

She put her hand back on his arm, well aware of the way it would make heat run up her arm and her skin tingle. She was ready for it. She was prepared for it.

"Maybe it's time to start." She hesitated for a moment. If she waited to see how he would react she might never continue. "So, why do you cover in a pediatric unit, Evan?"

She held her breath and watched as his pupils dilated ever so slightly, and he leaned toward her, closing the space between them.

"So, we're going to have those kinds of conversations?" It was a simple enough sentence. But it meant much more than those few words.

She took a deep breath. "I think we should try."

There. She'd said it. She'd taken that giant step. What did it really mean?

Evan was as cool as a cucumber. His eyes were steady. If he stayed still much longer she would start to count the flecks in his eyes.

He blinked and straightened his shoulders.

"I trained in pediatrics before I joined the DPA. My friend Tyler is a doctor at the Memorial Hospital in Atlanta. He's had skin cancer these past few months and needed surgery and treatment. I've been covering some of his shifts."

"As well as working at the DPA?" She was surprised. To be truthful, it was the last thing she'd expected. Why did she always think the worst of him? It was hardly fair. She was trying to hide the fact that her skin had just prickled when he'd said the name. Atlanta Memorial. The same hospital where she'd had her daughter. It was almost as if just when she'd decided to move forward, reminders kept popping up everywhere.

He shrugged. "He's my friend. His job's important to him. It felt good to work with kids again—to keep my clinical skills up to date. I'm not the bear you think I am, Violet. There's nothing like working with kids to bring you back down to earth."

Her throat felt dry, her mouth parched. She ran her tongue along her lips. The world seemed to have gone quiet around them. All her focus was on Evan and the diminishing space between them. It was all that seemed important right now.

"I don't think you're a bear, Evan," she whispered.

His hand rested on her hip. "So what *do* you think of me, Violet? Because I really don't have a clue. I can't read you at all."

His face was only a few inches a way from hers. She could sense the sizzle in the air. And for the first time it didn't frighten her at all.

The edges of her mouth turned upward. "I'm still trying to figure that out." She lifted her hand

and placed it on his chest, feeling the rise and fall of his breathing. She couldn't take her eyes off his. It was if he was hypnotizing her, drawing her in.

His voice was deep, husky. She could tell he was as affected by this as she was. "I've kissed you before, Violet. And you've never mentioned it since then. Do you even remember it?"

A whole host of prickling sensations swept over her skin. Did she remember it? Was he crazy?

"I remember every second."

His finger touched the side of her face. "Even though you were drinking?"

"Even though I was drinking." She tilted her head toward his hand, willing him to touch her some more.

This was a totally different experience from the last time. There was no alcohol to make her bold, to make her act out of character and be swept up in the moment.

She couldn't use alcohol as excuse for her behavior here.

He bent a little lower. She could feel his warm breath on her forehead, a smile dancing across his lips. "I'm going to kiss you now, Violet. Because I can't stop myself. Are you okay with that?"

She couldn't wait a second longer. She slid both palms up his chest, wrapping her hands around his neck and pulling him closer. "I think I can live with that."

And then his lips touched hers. Gently at first, a sweet and tender kiss. It was perfect. It was inviting. It made her want more.

She didn't feel threatened. She didn't feel scared. All she wanted to do was kiss him some more.

She took the final step, closing that last inch between them. Her body pressing up close to his.

She could feel his body awakening, just as she could feel her own doing the same thing. Their kiss deepened, his tongue gently probing into her mouth, willing her to separate her lips and give in to his demands. Her fingers slid through his short hair. Nothing had ever felt this good. Not even that last kiss.

This was better. This was more real. Every part of her body was awakened. Reacting to his touch and his responses. Everything about this felt good and so right.

His hands slid around her hips and cupped her bottom, pressing her even closer to him. Even though they were still kissing she could feel herself smile at his natural response. It made her feel in control. It gave her confidence.

His mouth pulled away from hers, moving along her chin and down her neck. This wasn't enough. This could never be enough. She wanted more and she wanted it now.

She could almost feel her heart rate quicken and her breathing change, her body preparing her for something else.

Something she hadn't even considered.

"Evan?" she murmured.

"Yeah?" His head was still down at the side of her neck.

"How long will it take us to get back?" She held her breath.

He straightened up immediately, his pupils dilating even further. He looked at her carefully, as if he was considering the implication of the question. His scrutiny made her lower her eyes. She was beginning to feel a little embarrassed. Her emotions and desire were clearly on display. What if he didn't feel the same?

He curled his finger under her chin, lifting her head back up to meet his. He was smiling at her. That lazy, sexy smile that drove her crazy. Most of the time he didn't realize he was doing it. But right now he was concentrating it on her, with full effect.

And the effect was dazzling.

He bent forward and whispered in her ear, his free hand capturing hers and intertwining their fingers, "Dr. Connelly, are you suggesting what I think you're suggesting? Because if you are, I'm about to hire a helicopter to get us back in two minutes flat."

Every hair on her body stood on end. His voice was so darned sexy. She smiled to taunt him a little more. "Make no mistake about what I'm suggesting, Dr. Hunter, and a helicopter is definitely required."

He gave her one final kiss on the tip of her nose then pulled back. "Let's finish our work here."

It brought her to her senses. Evan disappeared back inside the house. But she stayed outside. The sun was starting to set.

She should be feeling nervous. She should be feeling scared. The last time she'd had sex she'd been pregnant and still in a relationship with Blane. Evan would be the first person she'd slept with since the death of her daughter.

She lifted the hand that had held his and touched it with the other hand. She could still feel the warmth in her palm from where his fingers had intertwined with hers.

She wasn't scared. She wasn't. She was ready. And if he didn't reappear soon, she might drag him out of that house like a cavewoman.

Evan appeared at her shoulder. "I've got the blood sample. Jaja will meet me back here the day after tomorrow. We should have the results by then and be ready to do the lumbar puncture." He watched her for a second, obviously worried that the past few minutes had changed her mind. "Violet?"

He held out his hand toward her.

She didn't hesitate. "Let's see how fast you can drive." She slid her hand into his and pulled him off toward the truck.

CHAPTER EIGHT

THE JOURNEY SEEMED so long. Olibasi seemed oblivious to the sexual tension in the air and chattered away merrily about some of the families that they'd come into contact with that day.

Violet fixed a smile on her face, nodding at the appropriate times, all the while aware of the fact that Evan kept giving her sidelong glances. The tension was killing her.

When they finally reached the drop-off point for Olibasi and she slid out of the truck, the sigh of relief from the two of them was obvious.

They waited for a few seconds as Olibasi gathered up her colored skirts, gave them a cheerful wave and walked back to her village.

Their own was only ten minutes away.

"Well?" Evan raised his eyebrows at her, his voice laden with innuendo. "Have you changed your mind? Have you come to your senses?" Although his eyes were twinkling, she could almost hear the wariness in his voice—as if he was expecting her to run in the other direction.

She slid across the seat and put her hand on his firm thigh. "I can't tell you much about my senses right now, they seem to be going haywire."

It was almost as if she'd lit a match under him. He hit the gas pedal with a thud and the truck sprang forward instantly.

She moved her fingers in small circles over his thigh. He gave a little groan. "Not wise, Violet. Not wise at all."

"Really? Why ever not?" She was enjoying teasing him. She was enjoying feeling in control.

He lifted one hand from the wheel and pressed it down firmly on top of hers. Stopping her fingers in their tracks. "Five minutes," he growled.

She shuffled her shoulder closer to his. "Seems like an awful long time."

"Violet." He gave her a sidelong glance. "You're driving me crazy."

She felt something wash over her. A real feeling of contentment, a moment of pleasure. "Good, it's about time."

"What do you mean?"

"Working with you for the past six months has been an absolute nightmare."

His mouth quirked into a smile. "I'm hoping that's a good nightmare and not a bad."

She lifted her hand and touched the side of his cheek. It felt nice to finally touch him. She couldn't pretend she hadn't thought about it. She couldn't pretend that she hadn't done it in her dreams often enough. "It's been a torturous nightmare."

"You've still not told me if that's good or bad. And this from the woman with the slinkiest red dress in the world."

She felt her cheeks flush a little. He'd remembered. In the midst of the smallpox crisis he'd remembered her dress. "That was a distraction technique," she admitted.

"Well, it worked. Like a charm."

The truck ground to a halt outside their accommodation. Evan was out of the truck in an instant, pulling her door open and holding his hands out to capture her waist and lift her to the ground. He held her tightly for a few seconds. "Last chance, Violet."

She shook her head. "I don't need it."

There were a few people still around, still working and coming in and out of the clinic building next door. Evan murmured responses to their greetings as he pulled her along behind him. Pausing for a second, he ducked into one of the supply closets.

"What are you doing?" Violet hissed. She could feel the tension building inside her. There were several people around, all looking as if they might try to engage her in conversation at any moment. Talking was the last thing she wanted to do right now.

"Nothing." Evan came back outside, his hand stuffed inside his pocket. "Let's go."

"Evan, can you—?"

"Later." He dismissed the person holding a clipboard with a wave of his hand.

Violet suppressed a smirk. Evan never usually did things like that. Did he realize he'd probably just set tongues wagging?

But his strides were getting longer as they headed into the accommodation. More determined. He stopped as they walked in the main entrance, turning to face her. "Your room or mine?"

She pretended to think about it, putting her finger on her chin. "Hmm, decisions, decisions."

But Evan had obviously run out of patience. "Dammit. Mine is closer."

He pushed open a wooden door near them and pulled her into his room, thudding the door closed and sliding the bolt.

There was no time to look around at his room. No small talk. No hesitant moves. Violet found herself pressed up against the door. "So, where were we?" He had that sexy smile and lowered eyelids look. The one that drove her secretly crazy.

She slid her hands around his neck and stood on tiptoe, which allowed her to place some kisses on his neck. "I think we were right about here."

His hands settled on her hips, his full weight pressing against her. "So what's changed, Violet? What's changed for us?"

Was this a conversation she really wanted to have? Or did she just want to lose herself in the heat of the moment, because that's how good things felt right now?

"Apart from the increased dose of chemistry?"

She concentrated on Evan, running her hands

across the broad planes of his shoulders. She'd spent the past few months watching these shoulders from the other side of the room. Willing herself to forget what they'd felt like under her hands. Trying to erase all those thoughts from her head.

Because remembering had just made her want it all again.

And now she finally had it.

"Violet?" He wasn't going to give this up. He wanted to pursue why nothing had ever happened between them. Why, after they'd kissed, the next time she'd seen him she hadn't even looked him in the eye.

Her hands slid down the sides of his defined waist. She would have to ask him later whether he was a surfer. Maybe she'd do that when she'd finally got him naked.

Her hands inched lower, moving across his stomach, making the muscles twitch because he knew the inevitability of where she was heading.

He grabbed one hand and pinned it against the door, above her head. "Violet? Distraction techniques again?" He was teasing her, but she could see the questions in his eyes.

Was he afraid? Afraid that she was doing something she might regret and it could come back to bite him? Because she'd threaten to expose him a few weeks ago to the director? And it didn't matter that she hadn't meant it. He thought she did.

She bit her lip and looked him in the eye. Her other hand hesitated over the button of his chinos. "I wasn't ready."

It was as much as she could say. And it sounded so simple. Something that could easily be brushed over.

Because, right now, with her hormones swarming all over the place, the last thing she wanted to talk about was the stillbirth.

The last thing she wanted to acknowledge was the fact she'd had no sexual contact since it had happened. Just one passionate kiss with *him*.

She didn't need him to psychoanalyze her to death. She needed him to sleep with her. She needed him to fulfill the unspoken promise he'd made when he'd kissed her and sparked a fire she hadn't felt in three years.

She saw something flicker across his eyes. He was contemplating stopping what they were doing. He was considering pulling back. *No!*

His hand had inched upward from her waist toward her breast. But it had stopped midway. "And are you ready now?" He looked as if it was taking all his self-control not to move.

"I'm ready." She flicked the button open on his chinos. *Distraction techniques? You bet ya.*

He let out a hiss as she slid her hand inside. "You'd better mean this, lady, because there's no turning back."

"I've no intention of turning back." She could feel the adrenaline coursing through her veins. This feeling might not last but she fully intended to embrace it while it was there. She hadn't let herself feel like this six months ago. She hadn't let herself let go.

Now it was time.

She smiled at him. "I take it this means you like me a little?"

He raised his eyebrows, "You can take it that means I like you a lot."

And the chemistry between them was leading her by the hand.

The air in the room was stifling. Claustrophobic. Or maybe it was their chemistry?

It was dusk; the early evening sun was vanishing, causing the dim room to be filled with occasional dark orange rays.

Something was making her want to get naked very quickly. And he obviously had the same idea because Evan started walking backward, pulling her toward the single bed. His fingers started tugging at her *buba* top, lifting the bottom and dragging it over her head. It hit the floor and he stopped for a second, taking in the sight of her pink-satin-covered breasts.

What was wrong? Didn't he think they were big enough? Was he disappointed by what he was seeing? How much could he actually see in this light?

Then a sexy smile appeared on his face, and his hands reached up and cupped her breasts. "You're beautiful, Violet. I've never got to tell you that before."

A wave of relief swept over her. But he wasn't finished. His hands pulled down her long skirt, leaving her in her pink satin underwear. She felt herself pulling her stomach in. Would he notice? She had a few stretch marks from when she'd been pregnant. And her stomach was gently curved. Nothing in the world would ever change that.

And she wouldn't want to.

But she couldn't take the questions right now—not when she was feeling so ready to take the next step.

Evan seemed to have missed her stomach. His eyes were fixed firmly on her legs. "Why am I the only one undressed here?" she said out loud.

She stepped forward, pushing him back to the edge of the bed and slowly starting to undo the buttons on his cotton shirt. He watched her, unmoving, taking a sharp intake of breath as she reached the last button and slid the shirt off his shoulders, bringing both her palms around and running them up and down his chest.

She was taking her time over this—she'd waited too long not to enjoy it.

The scattered dark curly hairs on his chest tingled against the palms of her hands. His nipples tightened and she loved the effect she was having on his body. She pushed him back on the bed and sat astride him. "How about you take something else off for me? It's a little hot in here, don't you think?"

She was making a rocking motion, feeling the hardness of him underneath her. It felt so good.

Evan took a few seconds to push his chinos down over his hips, kicking his shoes off and grabbing her hips.

There was very little between them now. And she couldn't wait for the inevitable.

Then something struck her and she froze. Why hadn't she thought of that earlier? They were out in the middle of nowhere. This could ruin everything.

"What is it? What's wrong?" Evan's brow was wrinkled. "Violet?"

She thudded her hands down on his chest in frustration. "I'm not on the Pill. And I don't have anything with me."

His eyes twinkled. "That's why I'm the team leader around here. I plan ahead." He reached down and grabbed his trousers, pulling out a strip of foil packets that unraveled and almost reached the floor.

"Condoms? You brought condoms with you?"

He shook his head. "What did you think I was getting out of the store? I didn't plan *that* far ahead."

Of course. It was one of the standard supplies they had in abundance. To prevent sexually transmitted diseases and unwanted pregnancies. She'd been so wrapped up in the polio work she'd forgotten about them.

She reached over and grabbed the strip. "Just how many did you plan on using?"

He grabbed her around the waist and flipped her over so she was lying on the bed beneath him. "It's the one thing we have plenty of around here." The strip was still dangling from her hand and he flicked it with his fingers. "These are all for you and me, baby. However long it takes."

She ran her hands up his chest again. "That sounds good to me. Now, where were we?"

"Right around here." He slid his hands over her breasts, releasing them from the confines of the satin cups. Her eyes fell on her dark pink nipples just as his head came down and captured one.

His tongue teased her as she writhed beneath him, his hand slid inside her underwear, teasing her some more. All of a sudden her underwear was too much. It was getting in her way.

His way and hers.

"I think we're a little overdressed," she whispered in his ear. "It's time to get back to basics."

"Your wish is my command." He smiled as he

snapped the clasp at her back and slid her panties down over her thighs. His boxers landed in a heap on the floor.

"Now, what exactly did you have in mind?"

Perfect. Just what she wanted to hear. She pulled his head down next to her mouth and started whispering in his ear again.

He raised his head. There was a wicked glint in his eyes. "Really?"

She nodded. "Really."

"Then let's get to work." His lips covered hers and she closed her eyes and let her previously secret dreams become a reality.

Evan should have felt on top of the world. The woman who had got under his skin months ago had finally ended up in his arms.

This was the point at which he should be walking around with a smile reaching from ear to ear.

But no matter how hard he tried, he couldn't keep a smile on his face.

Violet was currently his favorite person in the whole wide world. Here, in Africa, it was easy to push aside the issues he'd had with her brother.

It was easy to try and forget the way he'd felt.

But the gnawing ache in his stomach wouldn't leave him. Every touch of Violet's fair skin, every little smile from her seemed to send him hurtling into a vortex of guilt.

Violet was slowly but surely beginning to trust him. And that's what worried him most.

He was trying to forget the fact that he occasionally saw something fleeting in her gaze. Because right now he was praying it wasn't related to him.

He'd known from the minute he'd kissed her six months ago that he wanted to go further. This should be his perfect scenario. Out in the middle of nowhere, working on a task they both believed in, with no outside influences.

So why couldn't he sleep at night?

Why was the sight of Violet lying in his arms racking him with guilt?

Because deep down he knew he was going to have that conversation with her at some point.

He couldn't live with himself otherwise.

He was going to have to tell her his fears about Helen's death. That if he'd been more in tune with his team, he could have prevented it.

That would shatter anything that was building between them stone cold dead.

And the last thing he wanted to do right now was spoil it.

But it was eating away at him every day. He couldn't enjoy himself with Violet. He couldn't embrace the relationship the way he should because of the thought of what he had to do.

How would she feel about him then?

He didn't even want to think about that. He was acting like a coward. And that was one thing Evan Hunter definitely was not.

Two weeks had passed.

Two weeks of long days and even longer nights. He wasn't even attempting to hide to anyone that he and Violet were an item. Neither of them was waking up early in the morning to creep back to their own room. Violet sat beside him at most of the briefings, letting their hands brush and giving him little smiles.

She wasn't outwardly affectionate. That just wasn't Violet. But she wasn't employing any of her past avoidance tactics.

And it felt good. Or it would feel good if he could let it.

She was still a little closed off. She'd let him know very little about her past. He naturally didn't ask her about Sawyer. But she seemed quite private, only mentioning a couple of close friends and nothing about any past relationships.

If he could get his head round his own problems, he might eventually delve a little deeper. He stared down at her face. She was lying tucked under his arm, one hand on his chest. Her naked breasts were rising and falling peacefully as she slept. Her blond hair was fanned over his shoulder. And she looked so peaceful. So calm.

He really didn't want to do anything to wreck it.

There was gentle knock at the door. "Evan? I need to speak to you a minute, please."

He was instantly wide awake. No one had ever disturbed him at night before. It must be something serious.

He slid his arm out from under Violet and grabbed the nearest shirt and trousers he could find. He opened the door and took a step outside into the hall.

Ben, one of the Healthy World Federation members of the team, looked worried.

"What's wrong? Has something happened?"

He nodded. "We've had some news. There's been a report of an attempted kidnapping of a health worker in the next state. All organizations are currently reviewing the safety of their staff. You're wanted on the phone."

Evan felt his heart rate quicken. They'd been briefed about the dangers before they'd arrived. But so far nothing untoward had affected them.

He walked into the control room and took the satellite phone.

"It's Evan Hunter, what can I do for you?"

He listened for a few minutes, making notes and asking questions. "Where, exactly? Do you know who was responsible? Is there any indication that the trouble will spread? What about the safety of my team? No, no. There have been no signs of trouble locally. How often will this be reviewed? And the other team, have they been safely withdrawn? Yes, yes, I understand. Please keep me updated. Thanks."

He replaced the phone and stared at the wall in front of him. He hated to think that any health staff or community workers were at risk. Even though there was no immediate risk to his staff, the thought of anyone being harmed or in danger made him feel sick to his stomach.

Helen had been a friend—a colleague. And even six years on he hadn't learned to live with that guilt.

Was that the reason he'd never managed to form a decent relationship? It wasn't as if he hadn't tried. But six years was a long time to never manage more than a few dates at a time. To always wonder if he deserved to be living the life that one of his colleagues wasn't.

But what if something happened to Violet? He couldn't stand that. It didn't even bear thinking about.

Ben touched his shoulder. "What did they say?"

Evan shook his head. "I'll need to give a briefing to the staff later. The other team has been withdrawn. Shots were fired and attempts were made to kidnap one of the doctors. It was in the next state, but they're not sure if the conflict could spill over. We've got to be very cautious in the next few days. We need to make sure we know where everyone is, at all times."

He pointed to the equipment lying on the table next to them. "Everyone has got to wear one of the GPS transmitters. Usually only one of the team members needs one, but we're going to have to review that situation and make it clear."

Ben nodded. "Whatever you think is best, Evan."

Evan walked over the wall and looked at the maps. "We're going to change our pattern over the next few days. Leave the villages nearest the border. We'll concentrate on those closest to us, until we're sure the situation is under control."

His brain was whirring. It didn't matter that it was the middle of the night. He was instantly awake and there was no way he could go back to sleep now.

It was one of the joys of being a doctor. That instant adrenaline buzz in the middle of the night that kept you awake, even when your body was telling you it wanted to be tucked up in bed. It happened frequently as an intern, and constantly as you progressed up the scale.

His eyes focused on the wall. Was there anything else he could do? How else could he ensure the safety of his staff? Nothing else seemed to be jumping out at him. It was the best he could do for now. What he really wanted to do was ship

Violet out on the nearest plane, sending her back to Atlanta, out of harm's way.

But there was no way she would let him do that.

So he was just going to have to try and make things as safe as he could.

Because losing Violet just wasn't an option.

CHAPTER NINE

VIOLET THUDDED DOWN at the table. "What are you eating?" Her eyes were sparkling and her face flushed. Just the way she looked when was happy, or excited, or when they...

No. He had to stop thinking like that every time he was around Violet. It was becoming addictive.

He concentrated on the matter at hand. "Stew." He held up a forkful. It looked a little unconventional but the smell was great. "Where have you been?"

"On the phone." She grabbed a fork and scooped up a bit of his stew. "Yum."

"On the phone with who?"

The smile stayed fixed on her face. "Sawyer."

He winced. Sawyer again. The man was haunting his every move. For someone who had barely made contact with his sister—only the occasional call or text—for the past six years, he seemed to have renewed their connection with vigor. "What did he want this time?" He couldn't hide the tone of his voice. He would prefer never to hear Sawyer's name again.

Violet put the fork back on the table. He'd seen the flash in her eyes at his wince. She seemed to be taking her time before replying. Her cool green eyes met his. "Things are going well. The director has asked Matt to come back. He hasn't decided yet, but he'll need to make his mind up soon because Callie's handed in her notice."

Evan was shocked. Callie Turner was one of the most dependable doctors he'd worked with at the DPA. He couldn't believe she would want to leave. What had Sawyer done to upset her? It was instant—the thought that Sawyer must have something to do with this. Callie had always seemed happy at the DPA.

His stomach churned at the thought of having to work with Sawyer again every day. The thought of having a constant reminder of something he was doing his best to forget.

"What position has the director offered him?"

He was irritated. The director had shipped him off to the middle of nowhere and it sounded as if he was offering Matt Sawyer a tailor-made position.

Why couldn't Violet be someone else's sister?

Her voice remained steady but he could see something else going on behind her eyes. She shrugged her shoulders, "Consultancy. Lecturing. Whatever he'll agree to. Sounds like the director just wants to get him back on board."

She glared at him. "Why do you always automatically go against my brother? Callie and Sawyer are together. I didn't know this before, but Callie never wanted to work at the DPA. She had a sister who died in a car accident. They were going to work at the DPA together. I worked with Callie for three years and never knew that." She glared at Evan again. "Sawyer connected with Callie. He's given her the confidence to go after what she really wants—family practice."

"Callie Turner? Family practice?" He couldn't believe his ears.

"Yes, that's what she wants." Violet's voice had a determined edge to it. She was getting annoyed with him, but he couldn't help his responses.

Or maybe he didn't want to. This Sawyer thing

was always going to hang over their heads. It was always going to be the monkey on his back.

The thought repeated itself in his head again. *Why couldn't Violet be someone else's sister?*

It was beginning to eat away at him. It was beginning to find its way into all the good times he was having with Violet. Hanging over his head, waiting to crash down on top of them.

"And what does Sawyer get out of this?" It was still there. The hostility in his voice. Undisguised.

The expression on Violet's face changed. She looked off to the side. "A chance to be happy. A chance to have a life again." She sighed. "Everyone deserves a happy-ever-after, Evan. Even my brother."

She was mad. The words were gentle, but he could see the glint in her eye. Why did he do it? Why couldn't he just smile and nod glibly when she mentioned her brother?

Why couldn't he just forget about Sawyer and the fact he got all uptight every time he heard the name? Every time he remembered the circumstances they'd been in.

Every time he felt the guilt wash over him again.

But Violet had obviously reached the point of no return. "Enough is enough, Evan. I asked Sawyer about you, you know."

Evan felt his heart jump in his chest. "What? Why did you do that?"

"Because I want to bang your heads together. Neither of you will tell me what the issue is between you. Neither of you will really tell me what happened out there." She steadied her gaze and lowered her voice. "This can't go on, Evan. How can we have anything together when you seem to hate someone I love so much?"

She was right. He knew she was right. His animosity toward her brother was killing this relationship stone dead.

But what if he told her the truth? Surely that would just give them the same fate? "What did he say?" he mumbled.

"He said Helen died and he was angry. He said you both have some—" she held her fingers up "—unresolved issues."

Unresolved issues. Well, that was one way to put it.

This was conversation he couldn't have. This was a conversation he wasn't ready for. He stood up, pushing his chair away, and walked from the dining room, out into the early evening sun.

Violet's footsteps hurried out behind him. "What? What just happened? I don't get this. Will you tell me what went on?"

"Just leave it, Violet."

"No!" She was shouting now. "I won't leave it! Why won't anyone talk about this? What happened out there? You know what? Helen was my sister-in-law and I loved her. She was perfect for Sawyer and made him very happy. I thought he was set for life. I thought they would grow old together. And then this…" She flung her arms wide.

"This happens and everyone comes back close-lipped. My brother barely functioning. Well, you know what, Mr. Team Leader? I've had enough. Helen was my family and I have a right to know what happened out there." She poked a finger into his chest. "And I mean besides the fact that she had an ectopic pregnancy and died. I want to know the other stuff—the stuff that you and my brother won't talk about."

Evan couldn't listen anymore. Everything was building up inside him like a tidal wave. Every pent-up emotion, feeling and load of guilt that he'd ever experienced.

It was too late. He couldn't hold on to this any longer.

"He must have known! Sawyer must have known Helen was pregnant! He let her go out there and put herself at risk!" He was shouting now but he couldn't help it.

Violet's face paled. She looked shocked. "What? Why on earth would you think that? That's ridiculous."

"Really? This is Sawyer and Helen we're talking about here. I've never seen a couple so connected. So in tune with each other. How could he possibly not have known?"

Violet shook her head fiercely. "Are you crazy? Helen didn't even know—and if she didn't know, how could Sawyer?"

Evan crossed his arms across his chest. "I don't believe that. I've *never* believed that."

Violet started to get angry. "What do you mean, you never believed that? You think my brother and his wife deliberately put the mission in jeopardy? Helen knew she was pregnant but didn't tell anyone because she didn't want to be taken off the duty rota?"

When Violet put it into words it sounded ridiculous. But, then, he'd never been able to think rationally about any of this.

"Well, she and Sawyer never wanted to be apart. Would that really be such a leap of faith?"

Violet was furious. "Of course it would." She nearly spat the words at him. "This is Helen you're talking about, Evan. Did you really know her at all? How can you even think that?"

His mind started to spin. Why had he said anything at all? He should have kept his mouth shut. This couldn't end well.

Violet folded her arms across her chest. "Evan, do you keep a note of when I have my period?"

"What? Don't be ridiculous." The question caught him sideways. He knew exactly what she was implying.

"Why is that ridiculous? We've been sleeping together for a few weeks now. You mean you aren't marking it on the calendar? Why not? You obviously expected my brother to."

"Of course I didn't!" he snapped.

"But, in essence, that's what you're saying.

That my brother should have noticed that his wife had missed her period. They were both busy professional people. But you expected them to be counting up the days?" She shook her head. "I don't know anything about my sister-in-law's cycle. It wasn't the kind of conversation we used to have. But what if Helen had irregular periods? How could either of them have known she was pregnant? She would only have been two or three weeks late. Maybe she didn't even think she was late at all. Or maybe, with all the planning for the mission, it just hadn't crossed their minds."

Her voice tailed off. She was right. He had known Helen. He'd known her well and respected her. She would never have deliberately lied. Even to be with her beloved Sawyer. Deep down he'd always known that.

But that threw all his beliefs out of the window.

No, that threw all his *excuses* out of the window.

Finally, he had to stop blaming Sawyer. He had to stop pushing the blame onto someone other than himself.

He slid down the wall and put his head in his hands.

"Evan?"

He could hear that Violet was confused. He could hear by the tone of her voice. The way it had quieted. The way her anger had quickly dissipated.

He felt her hand on his wrist. She was kneeling down next to him. "Evan, what is it? What's wrong?"

Violet started babbling. Filling the air around about them. "No one knew, Evan. No one knew that Helen was pregnant. It was horrible. And I'm sure it must have destroyed you all. Knowing that if you'd been back home, chances are that Helen would have been fine. But it was one of those things you couldn't have known. It was one of things that no one could have predicted."

Her words cut him to the bone. She had no idea what she was saying to him. Her warm fingers were wrapped around his wrist. Her other hand was on the top of his knee. He had to tell her.

He couldn't keep quiet anymore. The guilt was going to eat him alive.

But telling her would destroy any chance of them having a relationship. Any chance at all. How could she have a relationship with the man responsible for her sister-in-law's death? The man who could have made a difference?

Things could be so different for Violet's family. Sawyer would still have Helen. Violet wouldn't have experienced an estranged relationship with her brother for the past six years. She wouldn't have had sleepless nights and days fraught with worry.

All because of him. All because he should have paid attention. All because he should have uttered a few words, asked a simple question.

It could have made the whole world of difference.

If only he'd done it.

He raised his eyes to meet hers. This was the most painful thing he would ever have to do. "I knew."

"What?"

This thing with her brother was never going to go away and she was getting tired of it. She was getting tired of pretending not to be relieved she finally knew where her brother was and what he was doing.

Her heart was singing for her brother right now. He'd finally met someone to put a little light into his life and she was very happy for him. What's more, he'd met someone she liked and respected. She couldn't have wished for anything more.

Except for Evan.

She'd finally moved on. She'd finally taken the step of having a relationship again. And for the most part, it was good. No, it was great.

Her stomach flipped every time she saw him, every time he looked at her. His smile made her think impure thoughts. His touch drove her wild.

And for the first time in a long time she felt good. Good about herself. Good about the world around her.

Hopeful.

Hopeful that there was still a life out there worth living.

It didn't matter that this thing with Evan might not last. It didn't matter that chances were they were using each other as a distraction while they were in Africa.

So, why this? Why now?

She just didn't get it. She didn't get the animosity he felt toward her brother. She didn't get any of this.

Her skin prickled. The hairs on her arms stood

upright. There was something about what he'd just said. The way he'd just said it.

"What do you mean, Evan? What do you mean, you knew? Knew what?"

She could feel herself instantly building a wall around herself. Her self-protection mechanism was kicking in. Telling her to run. Telling her this couldn't be good.

His eyes were hidden under his heavy eyelids. Struggling to look at her.

She couldn't breathe. She couldn't swallow.

"About Helen." His voice was so low, so husky. He struggled to get those two words out.

A horrible sensation went down her spine. She instantly pulled her hands back, drawing away from him. "You knew what about Helen?" The thoughts were starting to form in her brain. She was trying to rationalize what she'd heard. "You knew she was pregnant?" No. He couldn't have. It wasn't possible.

He shook his head.

"Evan. Look at me." She couldn't stand the way he couldn't look her in the eye. This wasn't the man she knew. Evan Hunter didn't shy away from anything. So why couldn't he lift his head from his hands to look at her?

The frustration was overwhelming her. She reached over and yanked at one of his hands. "Look at me!"

He raised his eyes. They were laden with regret and guilt. What had he done? Had there been some cover-up at the DPA? Was that why no one was talking?

She couldn't bear the thought of that.

"Helen. She told me she wasn't feeling one hundred percent."

"What?"

He stopped to swallow. "While we were getting ready for the mission. I was packing up equipment and checking the inventory. She told she wasn't feeling great."

"And what?"

He shook his head. "That's just it—and nothing. I wasn't paying attention. I had too much on my mind. I didn't think anything else about it."

"Let me get this straight. A team member tells you they aren't feeling great before you leave and you didn't ask them anything else."

The words were obviously sticking in his throat.

He nodded. He ran his hand through his hair. One of Evan's signs of frustration.

"What else did she say?"

"Nothing. She said nothing." He squeezed his eyes shut. "But I should have asked her. I know I should have asked her. If I'd stopped for a second, if I'd thought about it. Helen never complained. It was unusual. I should have asked her to think about it. Why she was feeling unwell. What exactly was wrong." He was wringing his hands together now.

Violet was running through things in her head. "What difference do you think that would have made? Helen didn't know she was pregnant. She'd already reported as fit for duty. She hadn't even told Sawyer she didn't feel well."

"Don't you think I know that?" His voice carried across the compound. "She didn't tell anyone! Anyone apart from me! And I did nothing!"

Violet flinched back as he shouted. This was turning into a living, breathing nightmare. He stood up and started pacing around, his feet kicking up the dust around them. She shook her head. Her brain was spinning. She couldn't understand all this.

"What difference do you think you could have made, Evan?"

He stopped pacing. "What?" His head was shaking, ever so slightly.

"She mentioned, in passing, that she didn't feel great. How could you, by asking her questions, have made a difference? I don't get it."

His face was becoming redder and redder by the second. In her heart she would have loved it if anything in the world could have made a difference to her sister-in-law's outcome but the reality seemed very different.

He held up his hands in frustration. "I should have stopped. I should have paid attention. I should have asked her if there was any possibility she was pregnant!"

"Why would you ask her that? Why would you even think that?"

"Because if maybe I'd considered it a possibility, she might have considered it a possibility!"

The words hung in the air between them. There was so much on the line here. He was exposing everything about himself to her. He was exposing his failings. His failings as a team leader and as a person. What man ever wanted to do that?

She tried to push her family loyalties aside but could feel herself torn. Was there even a shred of possibility that could be true? Would Helen really have stopped to think she might be pregnant if Evan had asked her a few more questions?

She needed to step back. She needed to step out of this situation. She needed time to think.

She lifted her head. It was hard to look at him right now. There was too much conflict here. The rational part of her brain came into play. "Did you ever stop to think that if you'd asked Helen if she could be pregnant, she might have thought you were being sexist? She wouldn't have thanked you for asking that question, Evan. If you knew Helen as well as I did, you would know she might even have been angry with you."

His voice was quiet. "She might also still be alive." He let out the biggest sigh. "An angry Helen I could have lived with. It's the dead Helen I can't take."

Everything was silent round about them. There was no one else around, it was just her and him.

In the heart of Africa even the insects seemed to have become quiet.

Tears prickled in Violet's eyes. The horrible realization that Evan might be right. If he'd asked Helen if she could be pregnant, would she have checked the calendar? Would she have stopped for a minute to consider it?

Might it have saved her life?

There were so many ifs and buts. There was nothing definite here. Just a world full of possibilities.

Possibilities that neither of them would ever know about, because the time had passed.

It was over. There was no time machine. There was no way to turn back the clock. How many other people felt like that? How many mothers whose child's hands had slipped from theirs moments before a car had appeared? How many doctors who had sent a patient home, only for them to come back later and die?

And for her, how many women who couldn't remember the last time they felt their baby move?

A never-ending list. A whole world of don't-knows. A whole lifetime of what-ifs.

Evan turned to face her, his hands hanging by his sides. Even with his large, broad frame he looked broken. "How can I live with this, Violet?

How can I live with knowing if I'd done a better job Helen might still be here?"

She couldn't speak. She couldn't find the words she should be saying to comfort him, to reassure him that it wasn't his fault. That it hadn't been his responsibility.

It would be so easy to apportion him the blame. But, then, that's what he'd done to her brother. He spent the past six years blaming her brother for this. Thinking that he'd known about his wife's condition and had let her go on the mission with them.

He'd turned his anger on her brother rather than on himself.

How wrong. How unfair. As if Sawyer didn't have enough to live with.

Now he was blaming himself. Finally.

And in her heart of hearts she wanted to blame him too.

But she understood better than anyone what it was like to feel saddled with blame. Every moment in the last three years she'd wondered if she'd done something wrong. Something that had affected her pregnancy and stolen the life of her baby.

She'd interrogated her life to the point of not being able to move forward. Every thing that had crossed her lips during her pregnancy, every tiny twinge, every action she'd taken, every time she hadn't slept well or felt grumpy.

Anything that she could have changed that would have let her baby live.

Let her baby be born the living, breathing daughter she'd dreamed of.

But she'd had to let it all go.

Because no matter what she analyzed it didn't change the outcome.

It didn't change the results of the autopsy by the medical examiner. It didn't give her a reason for her daughter's death.

Because there had been no reason. Or none that could be found.

And no matter how hard it was, putting it behind her was the only way to start to move on.

Sometimes there just was no one to blame.

Her throat was dry. The dust in the air around her was stifling, or maybe that was just how she was feeling, as if the whole world was closing in on her again.

She tried to find some words. It didn't matter how much of a struggle it was to say them.

"You have to realize that Helen was a professional. You have to realize she was responsible for her own well-being. You have to let it go." Her voice was breaking now.

"But how? How can I let it go?" He reached toward her hand. She didn't want him to touch her. She wanted him to leave her alone. "Can you forgive me?"

His eyes were pleading with her. She could see how much this had destroyed him. She could see how much this had been eating away at him.

But she was so mixed up right now. Feelings of guilt and responsibility were rushing to the surface and she didn't feel equipped to deal with them.

There was no one out here to talk to. No one who understood.

She couldn't deal with his feelings as well as her own.

She felt as if she'd just jumped back a dozen steps.

She needed time. She needed space.

She raised her eyes to meet his. "It's not my forgiveness you need, Evan. It's your own."

And she turned and walked away before he could see her tears start to fall.

CHAPTER TEN

VIOLET LOOKED AROUND the village they'd just been arrived at. It was the third one they'd visited that day. She was trying to ensure all the local midwives were enrolled in the midwife service scheme and the oral polio vaccine pre-placed in delivery rooms to ensure administration immediately following birth.

She'd barely been in Evan's company since that fateful night two weeks ago. She just couldn't find the time and space to deal with him.

Because he'd brought so much to the surface again she was finding this task harder than she'd first thought. She was feeling raw and exposed.

And dodging Evan Hunter had become her number one priority.

She looked around. This was one of the bigger villages, with over two thousand residents and a mixture of midwives and traditional birth attendants. The birth rate was high, as very little form of contraception was used in the village and some of the expectant mothers from neighboring villages even came here to give birth.

Violet could hear some noise coming from the delivery room that was used in the village. She walked over hesitantly, unwilling to disturb the midwife if she was dealing with an expectant mother. Many of the births were attended by female family friends as well as the midwife or birth attendant, so Violet's presence might be considered intrusive.

As she approached the doorway the first thing she noticed was that, apart from Urbi, the midwife, only one other person was with the expectant mother. She was obviously in hard labor and her moans could be heard from the road, but what Violet hadn't heard was the fact she was also weeping quietly.

A horrible sense of dread came over her straight away.

Urbi looked up. She was using a traditional midwife's Pinard to listen to the baby's heart and waved her hand at Violet to come inside.

"Ah, Dr. Violet. Can you listen for me?"

Violet tried her best to remain calm. "Is there a problem? Where are the rest of the family?"

Urbi shook her head. "I sent them away. Hasana has been in labor for more than twelve hours. I haven't been able to hear the baby's heartbeat for the last hour."

No. Violet felt a shiver go down her spine. She wanted to turn and run away. She wasn't specially trained in obstetrics. Her fundamental knowledge was basic at best. How much use could she really be?

But the look on poor Hasana's face was desperate. And Violet's heart went out to her. She would be hoping, praying that Urbi had made a mistake. With every breath she would be willing that Violet would be the person to find her child's heartbeat.

The coiled-up feeling in Violet's stomach made her feel sick. She had to do her duty as a doctor. This birthing room wasn't equipped with the latest technology. There was no sonogram. No fetal Doppler, no fetal monitor. The only piece of equipment was the Pinard horn, the most fundamental listening device to detect a baby's heart.

Violet took a deep breath. There was no running away from this. She couldn't find any suitable excuse not to do the task she'd been asked to. As a doctor, she had a duty of care. "Is there any possibility that the baby has turned into an awkward position?"

Urbi had her hands on the mother's stomach. Her eyes were sad. She was one of the most experienced midwives that Violet had met since she'd arrived in Natumba state.

Violet was grasping at straws here and she knew it.

But she knew this situation better than anyone. She'd had the experience of being that mother. It took all her strength and self-resolve not to run and hide away in a corner. She really didn't know if she could go through this again.

Urbi spoke a few words in Hausa to the expectant mother. She looked back at Violet. "She felt her baby move last night when her labor started. The movement continued for the first few hours. There's been nothing since."

Violet pulled her ordinary stethoscope from her bag. She already knew this would be a futile exercise. "Let me try both of these," she said, taking the Pinard from Urbi's hands.

Hasana was tightly grasping the midwife's hand as Violet placed her hands on her stomach. The tightness of the grasp turned her knuckles pale.

Violet felt Hasana's tight abdomen first to determine the position of the baby. She'd used to do this to herself on a regular basis. It felt good to know which way her baby was lying at different points in the day.

Once she'd determined the baby's position she placed her stethoscope on the abdomen at the point where she should be able to hear a heartbeat. Her chest felt tight. She could feel Hasana's anxious eyes burning a hole into the side of her head.

"Has Hasana got any other children? Does she have any medical conditions?" The questions were rudimentary. They weren't going to change the outcome. But Violet felt she had to go through all the steps methodically.

Urbi shook her head. "This is her first. She has no medical conditions. There have been no problems during the pregnancy."

Something twisted in Violet's gut. It could be her they were talking about. No past history. No previous births or complications. A textbook pregnancy. No signs or cause for alarm.

She took the stethoscope from her ears and switched to the Pinard. She waited as Hasana was struck by another contraction and once it subsided she placed the Pinard on Hasana's abdomen in the hope something might have changed.

She was met with deathly silence.

Her eyes met Urbi's. "What have you told her? Does she understand English?"

Urbi shook her head. "Only a little. I will translate for you, Dr. Violet. I have already told her that I couldn't hear the baby's heartbeat. That was when I sent the family away. She knows I was just asking you to check again—to confirm what I suspected."

Violet nodded. Her brain was having flashbacks. Her own delivery room couldn't have been more different from this birthing room in Africa. Hers had been white, bright and modern with all the technology in the world. That hadn't made a bit of difference to her baby.

The gel being squirted on her stomach. The Doppler unable to find a heartbeat. The change of position. The blank looks on the faces of the delivery room staff—aware that she was a physician and would know exactly what they were doing.

Finally, her obstetrician speaking to her in low, gentle words. The progression of labor. The pain and frustration of knowing that there wouldn't be a euphoric and happy moment at the end. Her mind filling with the preparations she'd made at home. A bassinet, a stroller, a car seat and drawer after drawer of tiny little clothes.

The bright, colorful letters spelling out the name she'd chosen for her daughter on the nursery door. How could she go back home to all that without her daughter?

She lifted her eyes to meet the dark eyes of Hasana. She had a job to do here. And as much as it pained her, because she understood, she realized she might be the best person to do this job.

She took a deep breath and reached out for Hasana's free hand. She shook her head and spoke slowly. "I'm so sorry, Hasana, but I can't find a heartbeat for your child. Your baby isn't moving. I think your baby is going to be born asleep."

She hated the word *stillbirth*.

She couldn't explain why. It just sounded so cold. So distant.

For some reason, to her, a baby being born asleep sounded easier. Even though she knew the reality was that nothing could make it easier. She wasn't going to keep talking. She wasn't going to bombard Hasana with anything else.

She wasn't going to tell her she couldn't give her a reason why this had happened to her baby. She wasn't going to tell her there was no reason that she couldn't have a healthy child in the future.

Because right now this was all about this baby. Hasana still had at least an hour of labor to go through.

A first labor. A long labor. And what should have been labor of love had turned into a labor of sorrow. And in that moment Violet knew. She wasn't going to go anywhere. She was going to stay right here and hold Hasana's hand. It was one thing she was absolutely sure of.

Urbi translated her words. Another labor pain gripped Hasana's body, the tightening of her abdomen apparent. But her sobs were reaching far and beyond the labor pain. The noises she was making sounded like her very heart had been ripped out of her body. Her friend kept her arm wrapped around Hasana's shoulders, holding her close and letting her sob. Silent tears dripped down her cheeks as she tried to be strong for her friend.

Violet put her hand on top of Urbi's. "If it's all right with you, I'll stay. I've got some experience in this. I'll help you."

Urbi nodded her head. "Thank you, Dr. Violet." Her dark eyes watched her carefully. "Most people want to leave the birthing room when they know there isn't going to be a joyous celebration at the other end."

Violet could feel the tears pooling in her eyes. She had to stay strong. She had to stay professional. It was the best way she could support Hasana. "Every baby's birth should be celebrated, Urbi, no matter what the outcome."

Urbi's head tilted to one side, her years of experience very evident. It was almost as if she was reading Violet like an open book. Instantly understanding all the secrets she'd kept hidden away for the past three years. She wrapped her hand tightly around Violet's and gave it a little squeeze. "You are a good woman, Dr. Violet. May the Lord bless you."

There was a loud noise outside. Indistinguishable.

Urbi started. She spoke rapidly to Hasana then turned to Violet. "Let me go and check what that was."

She disappeared in a sweep of skirts, the dust clouding around her. Violet peeked out of the door in curiosity. Had a car backfired?

She could see people coming out of the houses surrounding them, all walking in the direction of the noise. Men were shouting at their families to stay inside. Urbi was nowhere in sight.

A horrible sensation started to sweep over her, a real prickling of unease.

She ducked her head back inside, holding Hasana's hand through another contraction. She pulled a pair of gloves from her bag and signaled to Hasana. "Can I check?"

The language barrier appeared to have disappeared. She knew exactly what Violet wanted to do. Violet did an internal examination and found Hasana was fully dilated. Any time now the baby's head would start crowning.

She pulled her hand back just as her brain realized what the noise outside was. Hasana let out a little shriek.

Gunfire. That was definitely gunfire.

Panic. She instantly felt sick. Adrenaline started coursing through her veins. The fight-or-flight response had never been so obvious.

In the distance she could hear voices shouting, followed by gunfire. What on earth were they in the middle of?

Hasana's female companion darted outside. Where was she going? Was she leaving them?

Violet tried to remain focused. She had to make a decision in the next few seconds. Hasana might be able to move in the next few minutes, but once she started crowning it would be virtually impossible.

She had no information to go on. How on earth could she assess their safety, their risk? And where on earth would they go?

Her heart thudded in her chest. For the first time in two weeks she wished Evan was by her side. She didn't feel strong. She didn't feel ready to deal with anything like this.

The voices were louder now. Fear started to

grip her chest. There had been reports about attempted kidnappings, bomb threats and health staff being slain.

All their intelligence had told them it was in the next state. There had been nothing to indicate any trouble at all near here.

But could she wait and take that chance?

What would Evan do?

Hasana's friend reappeared. She tugged at Violet's arm. "Go. Now. They are looking for you."

It was like all her worst fears realized. Her head went from one woman in the throes of labor to the other tugging her arm and pleading with her to leave.

"What about the rest of the team?" She might be the only doctor, but there had been four other community workers with her today. Where would they go?

Now she knew.

Now she understood what it felt like to have responsibility for the health and wellbeing of team members. Who to leave at risk—the staff or the patients? How on earth could someone make a decision like that?

"The villagers will hide them." It made sense.

The community workers were all from surrounding areas and all had dark skin and wore traditional dress. As long as their equipment was hidden they could easily blend in. Her blond hair and pale skin would make her stand out like a sore thumb. It would put everyone at risk.

Hasana managed to stand up and gripped her other arm. "I need you. Please." For a woman who couldn't speak or understand much English, her words were crystal clear.

She'd never felt so conflicted. Evan had given them all clear directions if they encountered any hostility. *Don't hesitate. Get out.*

But her Hippocratic oath was bouncing around in her head. She had a duty of care to Hasana. She had to help her.

And Evan wasn't here. No matter how much she wanted him to be.

She darted around the room, picking up the few things she thought she might need. Bags, gloves, the polio supplies to hide and a few blankets. Her brain was frantically trying to formulate a plan. The truck. Evan had said always to head toward the truck. It was their guarantee of getting out. Their safe passage back to camp.

But the noises sounded as if they were coming from that direction—the compound where they had left the truck.

Then she heard it. A loud, screaming woman's voice. Urbi. And straight away she knew why. She was making as much noise as she could. Obviously to try and warn Violet to get out.

Her voice was up against another, a male voice shouting back. Their dialogue was a mixture of English and Hausa. "The doctor left this morning," Urbi was shrieking.

Violet headed for the door, dropping the things that she held haphazardly in her arms. "Leave them," Hasana's friend hissed as she scrambled about the floor, grabbing what she could.

Her bag. Her satellite phone. But she had no time. The voices were only a few houses away.

Violet slipped her arm around Hasana's waist, ducking her head, and they made their way as quickly as they could between the houses. She had no idea where she was going. All she knew was that she couldn't head toward the truck.

A figure stepped out in front of them, causing her to gasp in alarm.

The dark-skinned Fulani man in traditional

dress silently pointed his finger in one direction. She'd vaccinated his children earlier.

She nodded in acknowledgment and hurried in the direction he pointed. It only took a few seconds to realize he was sending them out of the village and into the nearby hardwood forest. Plenty of cover for both of them.

They stopped for a few minutes as Hasana was gripped by another labor pain. She held on to a nearby tree trunk until she'd breathed her way through it. The voices were coming nearer. Closing in on them.

It was the most terrified Violet had ever been. She didn't know if she was more scared for Hasana or for herself. What would they do to Hasana if they caught her with the doctor? Would it actually be safer to leave Hasana behind?

No.

Hasana needed her right now. And she couldn't imagine abandoning her—not even for a second.

They stumbled through the forest, moving away from the thinner trees on the outskirts and into the darker depths. She felt herself drop something again as she held on tightly to Hasana, helping support her, but didn't dare look back to see what it was. They pressed on into the forest.

Violet kept glancing over her shoulder, praying that no one had noticed them and no one was following. She couldn't hear the voices anymore or the gunfire. That had to be a good sign.

She urged Hasana on. What she really wanted right now was her satellite phone. If she'd had it she could have phoned Evan and he could have arranged to get them out of here and get some support for Hasana.

In her head she could see it lying on the floor of the birthing room. Going back for it might have cost them their lives. No phone was worth that.

Hasana crouched down, her labor obviously progressing. They were near a mound of dark moss. Violet spread a blanket across it and urged Hasana to sit down. She pulled some gloves from her pocket and checked her again.

But she didn't need to. Hasana's baby was almost crowning.

Violet raised her eyes skyward and started some silent prayers. Please don't let them be found—they couldn't move now.

Please don't let there be any birth complications. It was too late to save the baby. But Hasana's life could still be at stake here. Hemorrhage, abruption, there could be whole host of delivery complications that could risk Hasana's life. And she was hardly equipped to deal with them.

She gestured at Hasana, signaling when to push and when to relax. Hasana's sobs grew louder. She didn't have her friend's hand to hold any more. She didn't have anyone other than Violet to support her. And they both knew what would happen next.

Evan was staring at the calendar, counting the number of days until they could head back to Atlanta.

What on earth would he say to the director once he got there? The polio program was likely to be a success. But his teamwork? His professionalism? His relationship with Violet?

Strike one. Strike two. Strike Three. Out.

It didn't bear thinking about.

Violet had barely spoken to him for the past two weeks.

And he couldn't blame her.

It didn't matter that her last words had been

about forgiving himself. She couldn't really have meant that. Not after what he'd told her.

It was no wonder she didn't want to be around him. He didn't want to be around him either.

He knew that she'd spoken to her brother a few times in the past two weeks. Had she told Sawyer what had happened between them? Would her brother be waiting at Atlanta airport with a baseball bat? That was all he needed.

He'd told Violet that they had *unresolved issues*. And he was right. They did.

Violet had told him he needed to forgive himself. And he was sorting all that out in his head— truly, he was.

But in order to fully be at peace with himself, the one thing he was absolutely sure about was that he was going to have to speak to Sawyer.

He didn't want to do it over the phone. He could have used the opportunity in the past few weeks when Sawyer had phoned to speak to Violet. But this was too big for Evan. Too important. He needed to do it face-to-face.

The way he should have done six years earlier, before Matt Sawyer had disappeared.

And he had to take whatever Sawyer dished

out because Violet was right about one thing. He couldn't live like this forever.

The phone next to him started ringing. He reached over and grabbed it. "Evan Hunter."

It was a hysterical babble. Not a single word made sense. It took him a few seconds for his brain to recognize the voice. "Jaja? Jaja, is that you?"

He stood up, the tone of his voice causing everyone around the room to stop dead.

"What is it, Jaja? Slow down, I can't make you out."

He gestured to one of the other team members. "Pull up the GPS signal."

He had six separate teams in different areas today, all working on the polio program. Where was Jaja working?

"What do you mean, gunfire? Who was firing? Where is the staff? Is any of the staff at risk? Are you safe?"

He was firing questions at Jaja and he knew he should take a deep breath and keep calm. The connection was terrible. He could hardly make out a single word. All he could gather was that there had been trouble in the village, shooting, and Jaja had barely made it to the truck in time to get out.

He started looking frantically at the papers on his desk, all describing the latest events in the neighboring state. There had been nothing about Natumba state. Nothing at all. He'd been advised to continue working. Had he just put his staff at risk? Had he sent them to an area where they could have been kidnapped? Or worse?

The bounty on a healthcare worker's head was huge.

The thought made him feel physically sick.

His brain was in overdrive. "What village, Jaja? Say it again. What village?"

He shouted the name across the room to the worker on the GPS system. "Who do we have there?"

Silence. The staff were waiting. Waiting to hear who was at risk.

The tension was almost palpable. Everyone seemed to be holding their breath.

The man sitting at the screen pulled up a table, covering the intensive GPS tracking system they used. His face paled. He rattled off the names—four community workers, Jaja among them. Then he hesitated and turned to face Evan. "And Violet." His voice was almost a whisper. Everyone knew about their relationship.

Evan could hear a roaring in his ears. His worst dream had just been realized. For a second time stood still. He felt as if he were in one of those slow-motion movie scenes. This couldn't be happening.

His legs moved automatically over to the screen. "Do you have the signals?" Beside him a hand picked up the phone, reporting back to headquarters, while another voice started shouting about pulling a team together.

The screen operator nodded, focusing the map on the village. From an aerial view there were five signals. One was moving away rapidly— Jaja.

Three others were unmoving, one slightly outside the village limits.

One of the local staff moved up next to his elbow. "The workers will be hiding. The villagers will have taken them somewhere. Somewhere they won't be recognized."

"Where's this? Where is this area?"

Evan's finger was stabbing at the screen. This

whole exercise was futile. Even though the workers all wore the GPS trackers, it only showed their positions. They didn't show a heartbeat. Didn't tell him if they were dead or alive. Didn't tell him if they were injured. Didn't tell him if they were safe or in danger.

And right now that was all he cared about.

The screen operator pulled up satellite images of the area surrounding the village. His face screwed up a little. "That looks like the outskirts, leading into the forest."

A forest. Cover. It could mean only one thing.

Evan felt a pull at his heart. "Violet. That's got to be Violet."

There was only one person who would need to head into the forest during conflict. One person who would be easy to spot in the village. He only prayed that Violet had headed into the forest of her own volition and not under duress.

The thought that entered his mind horrified him.

He pressed the phone next to his ear. "Come back here, Jaja. Right now. Don't stop. I need you to tell me everything you know." He turned to someone else. "How far away is that village?"

One of the staff members signaled him and said, "Headquarters say you've to stay put. You've not to go to the village under any circumstances. They will try and find out more intel for us. In the meantime, all staff are to start packing. It's likely they'll pull us all out."

Most of the faces in the room had paled. Imminent danger. That was the message from headquarters. They all knew what that meant.

You cleared out. You didn't go back for team members. This wasn't the military.

Evan let out a roar. His hand cleared the nearby desk of everything that was stacked on it. Several staff jumped out of their seats.

"I will not leave without Violet!" His voice filled the room, echoing in every corner.

He stormed out of the office into the corridor, his head pounding. *No. No.*

He couldn't lose another team member. He couldn't live with himself.

Not Violet. Not the one person in this world he couldn't live without.

It didn't matter if she hated him. It didn't matter if she never forgave him. He could live with that. He could survive. As long as he knew that Violet was somewhere else in the world and safe.

That was all he could think about. That was all he could focus on.

Luke, one of the team members, approached him. "I've got the other truck ready. We'll be ready to go in five minutes. We can meet Jaja *en route*. We can stop and get the intel we need from him before we get to the village."

"What?" He tried to focus. Tried to see beyond the rage that was currently invading his head. He couldn't believe his ears. Everyone had just been told to get ready to leave. The instruction had been clear. Everyone was to pack up and wait for the evacuation.

It didn't matter to the haphazard plan that was currently igniting in his brain. He couldn't ever ask any member of his team to do what he was about to do.

He could never let anyone risk their life for him, or for Violet. It was too much. Too much to ask of anyone.

He caught the dark arm next to him. "No, Luke. I can't ask you to do that. I won't ask you to do that. Pack up. Supervise the rest of the team. Wait for the call from Headquarters about the evacuation."

Luke shook his head ever so slightly. There was no emotion in his voice. "You didn't ask, Evan. You wouldn't ask. But I won't leave. I was in the military. I'm the right hand that you need. Now, let's go get Violet."

Evan couldn't breathe. There was an iron fist gripped around his heart. He couldn't let Luke do this with him. There was no way he'd be leaving without Violet, but the thought that another human being would knowingly walk into something they might not get back out of—for him, for Violet—was too much of a struggle.

His team leader instincts were screaming at him to keep everyone safe. He'd spent the past six years whispering that mantra to himself, ever since Helen's death. Team safety meant everything to him. Sometimes to the detriment of the role of the DPA. Evan would never let team safety be compromised again.

This went against everything he believed in. It went against everything he lived for.

How could he accept help? Pictures of Helen's weak body being held by her husband haunted his mind. His brain couldn't even comprehend the risk.

He shouted some instructions to the other members of staff—to communicate with the villagers, to leave supplies of everything, to pack only essentials, to keep in constant contact with headquarters.

People were rushing past him. "Do you have a portable version of that?" He pointed to the GPS mapping system.

The analyst nodded and pulled a laptop out of the wall. "It's fully charged. Press this and this. Refresh every five minutes."

They were all the instructions he needed.

He strode back out toward the truck. Luke had positioned himself directly in front of it. Directly in Evan's path. His large frame was blocking out the sunlight. "Ready?"

Evan hesitated. He was team leader. He should order Luke to pack and leave. But something was stopping him. Something was making him take stock.

And this wasn't about Violet.

This was about all the things in life that couldn't

be controlled. That *he* couldn't control. No matter how hard that was to accept.

Luke was making his own decision. A grown-up, adult decision to accompany a member of staff on a mission they might not return from. A mission to retrieve their colleagues.

He was an adult with his own free mind. Evan knew that if someone had told him he couldn't try and rescue Violet, he wouldn't have listened. Not for a heartbeat.

Why should Luke be any different? As a military man he probably understood the risks better than Evan ever could. But he was still here.

And in that instant Evan understood.

Understood that he had to accept the things he couldn't control. He had to let Luke make his own decision. He wasn't responsible for everything around him.

He was team leader. Not a ruler. Not a military commander.

He was one man. And there was only so much he could control. So much he could be in charge of. No matter how much he hated it.

And right now all of his thoughts were on Violet.

He extended his hand toward Luke. "Thank you. Thank you for your help."

Luke shook his hand swiftly. "Let's go."

They'd been in the forest for just over an hour now. Violet tucked her watch back into her pocket.

She had no idea what was going on in the village right now. Was everyone safe? She couldn't bear the thought that anyone from the village had been injured trying to protect and hide her and her team.

Urbi. What would have they done with her? Someone must have told them the midwife had been working with the American doctor. Would she be safe?

What about the men who had come into the village? Were they still there, waiting for her to re-appear? Had they been able to identify her team among the villagers?

She didn't even know what the men looked like. How many had there been? She'd only heard one voice. She'd heard the gunfire and the shrieks. Then the whispers that they were looking for her and wanted to kidnap her.

It was terrifying.

It didn't matter that she'd had safety briefings. She hadn't really believed they would be at risk. There had been no trouble in that area before and the truth was she'd always felt safe with the people in Natumba.

She hated that this had happened. She hated that this could put the polio program in jeopardy.

And she hated what this might be doing to Evan.

If it was possible, her blood would be running cold right now. He would be frantic—and in that state of mind there was possibility that he wouldn't act rationally.

Evan could put himself in danger—for her, and for the rest of the team, and she couldn't stand the thought of that.

She already knew that losing another team member was his greatest fear. She couldn't imagine the agony he was going through right now.

And he was the one person she wanted to talk to. It seemed almost ridiculous that she'd spent the past two weeks avoiding him. At any point she could have sat down with him and talked things out.

But no. She'd been too stubborn.

Her brain had still been mulling over what he'd told her. It had stung initially. That tiny second of deliberating whether he'd actually been to blame for Helen's death.

Of course he hadn't been. It was ridiculous.

But what was really obvious was that Evan had a way to go before he was ready to move on. She'd been deadly serious when she'd told him the first person he needed to forgive was himself.

She knew a lot about that.

She'd had a mountain to climb in order to forgive herself over her daughter's death. There was no blame to apportion and sometimes that made it all the harder to move on. To take the step forward to a new life.

She really didn't think she could handle someone else's unjustified guilt when she'd just managed to walk away from her own.

There was a rustle of leaves right next to them. She jumped and Hasana's eyes widened. She was in the grips of another labour pain—they were coming much quicker now—and she looked as if she wanted to cry out.

Hasana grabbed a piece of dry bark and pushed it between her teeth.

Violet felt as if she couldn't breathe because even taking a breath made a little noise that someone might hear. That could reveal their position.

She put her fingers silently to her lips, praying that Hasana wouldn't let a noise escape.

The leaves rustled again and Violet strained her ears. She couldn't hear footsteps. She couldn't hear voices. And somehow she didn't think these men would come through the forest quietly if they were looking for her.

The rustle continued. Then a small reptilian head appeared, followed by a body slithering along the ground.

A snake. The rustle had been a snake.

Violet didn't know whether to let out a sigh of relief or not. Was that type of snake poisonous?

She pointed with her finger and Hasana shook her head, gripping the tree bark with her teeth. A snake was the last thing on her mind right now.

Violet watched as the snake seemed to look in their direction once then slithered off without another glance.

Maybe bringing Hasana into the forest hadn't been such a good idea.

She waited for a few more seconds, listening for any other noises. But there were none.

She placed her hands on Hasana's belly. The baby was in the correct position. Its head had engaged and the labor seemed to be proceeding well. The baby was a good size. Maybe too big for a first-time mother?

Violet hoped not. She didn't have access to a theatre if an emergency Caesarean section was needed. She didn't even have access to a set of forceps if the baby's head became stuck on the way down.

Hasana was going to have to do all this on her own.

She checked the position of the baby again. The head was crowning. It was time for Hasana to push.

Something washed over her. She was about to face her greatest fear all over again. Only this time the pain wouldn't be hers, it would be someone else's. She had to be strong. She had to be strong for Hasana.

She had to push all her thoughts and fears aside. She had to get through this.

Stillbirths weren't unusual in Nigeria. But more than half of them occurred while the woman was in labor. Most happened in rural areas where skilled birth attendants or midwives weren't available.

That hadn't been the case for Hasana. But there were five major reasons for stillbirth. Childbirth complications, maternal infections, congenital abnormalities, fetal growth restriction and maternal disorders such as diabetes or pre-eclampsia.

Violet was running through all these in her head. The baby felt a reasonable size so there couldn't be a fetal growth problem. Urbi had told her there had been no complications during the pregnancy, so she was assuming pre-eclampsia, diabetes and maternal infections were not a possibility. There was no way to know if there were any congenital abnormalities—not until the baby was born.

Back home in the U.S. women were screened for congenital abnormalities and things were often picked by obstetricians doing detailed scans. But Hasana had had none of these tests available to her. They wouldn't be able to tell if something was wrong with the baby until he or she was born.

Hasana's muscles contracted tightly again—another contraction. And Violet held up her fists and scrunched up her face, miming pushing.

Hasana let out a cry, pushing with all her might. The time for being silent had obviously passed. The baby's head appeared between her thighs.

Violet's actions were second nature. It didn't matter that this baby was already dead. She'd gone back into junior doctor phase and was checking around the baby's neck for a cord. There was nothing there. Nothing restricting the baby's breathing. Nothing that could have led to its death.

Another push and the shoulders appeared, quickly followed by the rest of the slippery body. Violet caught the little baby in her hands, grabbing one of the blankets to wrap it in.

A baby boy. Hasana had a baby boy.

She wiped his little face. Praying against everything that he would breathe. But his pale lips against his dark skin showed that would never happen.

He was perfect. In every single way.

Her heart felt as if it could break all over again.

Hasana lay panting, exhausted after the delivery of her sleeping child.

There was no obvious congenital abnormality. No obvious reason for this baby to have been born asleep.

Just like hers. Just like her own daughter.

It didn't matter that nothing here reminded her of home and her own experience. It didn't matter that this forest floor was about as far removed from an Atlanta hospital as it was possible to be.

All that mattered was the perfect little boy in her hands. The little boy who should have been breathing.

She lifted him to her shoulder and held him for a few seconds. The umbilical cord was still attached, still making him part of his mother. She would deal with that in a few seconds.

She took a deep breath. Baby. New baby smell. It surrounded her in all its wonder. If only this moment could be different. If only she could be handing over a screaming baby to his mother.

She didn't care about the potential kidnappers in the forest. She didn't care about being silent anymore. She only wanted to will this little baby to life.

A single tear dripped down her face.

Life was so unfair. This little boy should be taking his first breaths. This little boy should be allowed to grow. He should have a life ahead of him.

He should be able to learn to crawl and to walk and talk. He should be part of a loving family. He should grow from childhood to teenage years, to adulthood. A life probably with intermittent hardships but a life worth living.

Instead, in her arms she had a silent, beautiful baby boy.

She helped Hasana sit up. She didn't have syntometrine to inject and help with the third stage of delivery. She was lucky to have something to clamp and cut the cord.

There was no one to translate for her now. Hasana spoke mainly Hausa, and she herself only English. But, here in the middle of the forest, they would have to muddle through.

She handed over the baby to Hasana. "You have a beautiful son, Hasana." She couldn't help the tears that fell down her cheeks. Hasana would think she was crying for her son—and in a way she was. She was crying for every sleeping baby that had ever been born. As only a mother could.

She wrapped her arm tightly around Hasana's shoulders, watching her embrace her little boy. She watched as Hasana dropped kisses on each of his eyelids and lifted his hands from the blanket and counted his tiny fingers.

It was almost as if she was embracing his perfection. The fact that in every way he looked like a healthy baby.

Her shoulders were racked with sobs and her tears soaked Violet's *buba* shirt. The light was beginning to dim among the trees. But Violet didn't want to pull her watch out and check the time.

Time here was more precious than anything. Hasana needed this time to spend with her son. To mourn his loss. To start the long grieving process that Violet knew inside out.

The hopelessness.

The despair.

The endless questions.

Everything would change once they returned to the village. Her family and friends would take over. Probably arranging a burial and blessing for the baby. Doing what they thought was best for Hasana.

But right now, right here, there was no need for any of that.

This was a time for mother and son to be together.

And although the rest of the world might not understand, this was the most precious time of all.

The one thing you could never get back.

And Violet had all the time in the world.

CHAPTER ELEVEN

LUKE PULLED THE truck over to the side of the road. "Now we go on foot."

Evan's eyes scoured the surrounding area. They hadn't reached the village yet but the last thing he wanted to do was announce their arrival.

They'd met Jaja on the road. He'd been hysterical and had wanted to come back with them. But it was obvious he wouldn't be of any use. He was jabbering incessantly and still shaking with fear. It had taken all Evan's self-control not to shake him by the shoulders to get some sense out of him.

Finally, they'd managed to find out a little more. The men had arrived in the village around 3:00 p.m. There had been four of them, all in one truck. They'd fired shots into the air and had demanded to know where the American doctor was.

Jaja had been on the other side of the compound, next to the truck in which Violet and the rest of the community workers had arrived. He hadn't had time to look for the others. He knew that Violet had been with the local midwife, Urbi, and the others working between houses in the villages. The armed men had been between Jaja and his colleagues. And as he'd jumped into the truck and sped away to raise the alarm, they'd fired at him. The evidence was all around the body of the truck.

Evan had quickly checked him over and sent him back to the camp. There was still no further information from headquarters.

"You know we should wait, don't you?" he said to Luke as they walked alone the edge of the dusty road.

Luke raised his eyebrow. "Are you going to wait?"

Evan couldn't meet his eyes.

"Then neither am I. But you do exactly as I say. I don't have a gun, we don't have any kind of weapon. We're going to skirt around the outside of the village and see if we can work out if the kidnappers are still there."

Evan glanced at his watch. It was nearing seven o'clock and the light was beginning to fade. The village was nearly ninety minutes away from camp, but the journey had seemed much longer.

His brain had computed a million possibilities in that time, most of which he didn't want to consider. He hated the way he kept falling on the worst-case scenario. He hated the way the rational part of his brain had ceased to function.

As their truck had sped along the dusty road he had kept praying someone from the village would make contact via the satellite phone but no one had heard a word. And they had no other form of communication.

In the shadows the outline of the village houses started to appear. Luke signaled him to get behind him as they crept slowly around the edge of the first house. Everything was silent. A quick glance told them no one was inside.

They worked their way systematically toward the center of the village. From the deathly silence on the outskirts they started to hear the gentle hum of voices. As they moved closer the noise level increased.

Evan tilted his head to one side as they strained to hear. "It sounds like panic," he whispered. "A lot of shouting, mainly in Hausa, with a little English."

Luke gave him a nod. "I'm going to get a little closer." He put his hand up as Evan tried to move behind him. "You're the doctor. Stay here. It will only take me a few seconds. Once I know for sure there's no one with guns, I'll signal you." His dark eyes flashed. "I mean it, Doc, don't move. There might be people in the village who need your help. I don't want you to get injured."

He moved away silently around the edge of one of the houses, virtually invisible in the fading light.

Evan strained to hear. The voices just sounded like a rabble to him. But there was no gunfire. No shooting. He hated having to stay here. His legs were itching to run—to run and find Violet. To make sure she was safe.

But if the kidnappers were still in the village, they would be only too happy to find another American doctor, and he knew that. Luke was right. He had to wait a few minutes and then see if any of the villagers needed attention. He knew all about his duty as a doctor. But what about his duty to Violet?

"Evan! Come out, you're needed!" Luke's deep voice cut through the dying light. Evan's blood started to pump and he ran toward the voice.

The noise around him increased rapidly. It seemed as if every resident of the village had made their way into the village center. That's why all the houses were empty and silent. There were several people on the ground. He recognized one of them immediately. Urbi. The village midwife.

He was at her side in seconds. Luke appeared at his shoulder. "The men left the village little over an hour ago. They couldn't find Violet. They searched everywhere."

One of the community workers touched Evan's elbow. Her dark face was filled with anxiety. "We had to hide Dr. Hunter. When the men appeared, we had no choice but to hide among the villagers."

Evan was examining the deep wound on Urbi's head. "What happened?"

"Urbi was knocked unconscious. She delayed the men from reaching Violet. She told them Violet had already left the village. They hit her with a rifle butt."

His stomach was clenching. Violet. This woman had been injured trying to save Violet.

He couldn't stop himself. His head flicked frantically around. "Where is she? Where is Violet?"

He took a pack of swabs from his bag and held them to Urbi's forehead. Her small hand reached up over his. "We don't know, Dr. Hunter. She must have heard me shouting. When they got to the birthing room she was gone. She was helping me with a patient." She winced as he tried to stem the flow of blood. "They discovered some of her things in the birthing room. She must have dropped them. That's when they hit me."

Evan's stomach flipped over again. "But they didn't find her?"

One of the other villagers was shaking his head. "No."

Luke was kneeling next to another man. His shoulder had been grazed by a bullet. Another seemed to have been punched and one of the village elders had a similar wound to Urbi's.

Evan looked around at these people—most that he didn't know—who had hidden his staff and saved their lives. "Thank you," he said. "From the bottom of my heart, thank you for looking after the health workers."

A hand appeared on his shoulder and a variety of items were deposited on the ground next to him. Violet's bag. Her smashed satellite phone. Some of the polio supplies.

The sight of her battered belongings in front of him tore at his soul. It was obvious why no one had been able to contact them. The men had obviously destroyed the satellite phone once they'd found it.

He cast his eyes over the patients. Luke was a physician's assistant in the U.S. There was nothing here he couldn't deal with. He stood up. "Luke, can you deal with these people, please? I need to look for Violet."

Luke nodded briefly. The danger was past. There was no reason for him to stop Evan.

"Urbi, do you have any idea where Violet could be?"

"She was with a patient. A villager who was in labor. They must have gone somewhere to hide."

"But where could they have gone?" His eyes took in the surrounding area. The uneven rows of houses around them. The backdrop of the forest.

The forest. The ideal place to hide a conspicuous white face.

Urbi's hand reached out to his. "Dr. Hunter—the patient…"

He knelt back down. "What is it? Was something wrong with the patient? Was that why Violet didn't leave her?"

Urbi's expression was guarded. She gestured for him to move closer so she could whisper in his ear. "The baby. It was too late for the baby. There was no heartbeat. But the mother still had to deliver it."

Evan nodded. Violet must have been worried about complications of delivery for the mother. That's why she'd stayed by her side. That's why she'd taken her with her.

But there was something else. Urbi pulled him a little closer. "Dr. Violet. She understood. Once she realized the baby was dead. She said she wanted to stay. She wanted to help."

Evan pulled back a little. Violet was a compassionate person. He didn't think she had much experience in obstetrics, and he knew there was a high stillbirth rate in Nigeria so she must have wanted to help.

"Please find them." She squeezed his hand.

Finding Violet was all he could think about right now—all he could focus on. Someone pressed a torch into his hand. "You might need this."

He stared down at the torch. The confusion in his brain didn't matter. The way that things were circling in his head didn't matter. There was movement beside him and he looked. A number of the villagers had formed a group around him.

His understanding was instant. In the poor light it would be difficult to find anyone in the forest. He had no idea how far Violet and the woman in labor might have traveled. It could be anything from a few hundred yards to as far as they had been physically able to.

Again, the people in this village were prepared to help. He was touched.

He drew his shoulders back. "Okay, Luke?"

Luke nodded. "No problem. I'll be waiting for you when you get back." The unspoken words were there. *When you get back with Violet.*

Evan nodded at the people around him. "Thank you. Thank you so much." They walked swiftly through the houses to the edge of the forest.

There, the villagers started to talk among themselves and split into groups.

He pulled out the laptop he'd been given and reloaded the GPS software. The little red blip on the aerial view was still evident. He held up the laptop so the people around him could see, showing the view of the forest and where the red blip lay. "That should be Violet," he said out loud. He tried to picture where they were on the map. "We need to head in that direction." It seemed as though Violet had veered off to the left and headed into the forest for about half a mile. A hard trek in these conditions—let alone with a pregnant woman in labor.

There were no obvious paths into the forest, no tracks leading in different directions. Several of the stronger men had brought stiff canes with them, obviously to beat back some of the thicker leaves and jagged bushes.

Evan took one that was being held out toward him. He watched as several others starting beating at the bushes in front of them, clearing a path into the forest.

He started doing the same. Several of the men followed him, their torches helping to light up the dark forest. Shadows and outlines seemed to loom everywhere. The noise of the insects around them increased with every step they took further into the forest. He started slapping at his skin. Mosquitoes. He hadn't even thought about insect repellent. By the time they finished they would be eaten alive.

The deeper they went, the denser the forest became. The ground around his feet seemed alive. Every step crunched on something underfoot. The trees were closer together now, their trunks thicker and leaves slapping around him. The distance between the groups was increasing as they spread out to cover more ground between them.

Evan wasn't really sure which direction they were heading in any more. The forest could be disorientating. Especially at night. How would Violet be feeling? Would she be scared? Would the patient be in trouble?

He stopped for a second, looking around, sweeping his torch through the leaves and bushes.

There was no point in pulling out the GPS software now. It was only useful if you knew where you were in relation to the signal. He could hear shouts around him. The other searchers were obviously getting disorientated. Was it safe to continue?

There was no way Evan was going back to the village without Violet. No way at all. "Violet! Violet!" He started shouting like the others, stopping every few seconds to listen for any response.

Nothing. Were they heading in the right direction? He started to move a little more left, his torch trying to find an easier path for their feet.

His shoulders and arms were aching relentlessly as he tried to beat the bushes and leaves back. At least Violet would have been able to see these in the daylight and duck out of their way. He could hear some muttering behind him. How long had they been out here? Were the villagers starting to lose heart?

His torch caught a glimpse of something unusual. A color he didn't expect to see. He dropped to the forest floor and scrabbled about. A notebook. Violet's notebook with the distinctive purple flowers. His heart leaped. They were heading in the right direction.

"Look! It's Violet's!" He showed it to the men behind him, who instantly shouted to the other groups.

His adrenaline surged. The pain in his arms was forgotten. She must be close. She must be nearby. "Violet! Violet!"

Every step had renewed vigor. His calls were louder than before. His shouts echoed through the forest. All the men were repeating them over and over.

Then he heard something. Something different. "Quiet!"

He stopped moving and held his breath.

Then he heard it. A hoarse reply. "Evan?"

He'd never heard anything sweeter.

He flung his stick aside, crashing through the forest toward the voice. He burst through into a little clearing. Dark moss, set among some trees. Violet huddled on a fallen tree trunk, her arm around another figure and a little wrapped bundle in her arms.

"Evan." The relief in her voice washed over him. Her pale face could be picked out easily in the dark night. He crossed the clearing in a couple of strides and pulled her into his arms.

"Are you all right? I've been so worried. No one knew where you'd gone." His eyes caught the woman to her right. "Did the delivery go okay? Is there something we can do for your patient?"

Violet shook her head silently. The men from the village had heard the shouts and crowded into the clearing. One of them rushed forward and took Hasana in his arms, shouting with relief.

Violet felt the tears on her face instantly. She laid a gentle kiss on the baby in her arms. She whispered to him, stroking the skin on his face as she talked to him a little longer.

And in that instant, Evan knew.

It felt as if a hand was squeezing his heart inside his chest. It was the tenderness, the look on her face. Pieces of the puzzle started dropping into place.

Violet was a good doctor—she'd always been a good doctor. But she'd risked her life to stay with this woman. She'd trekked through a forest to keep her, and a baby that she already knew was lost, safe.

Evan's skin prickled.

No. Not Violet. That couldn't have happened to Violet.

Things started to jumble around in his brain.

The look on Violet's face when he'd told her she would be working with the midwives.

He hadn't been able to place it at the time. Had it been fear?

Violet had seemed so at ease with the young children and the babies. Surely she wouldn't feel like that if she'd experienced a stillbirth? Surely she would want to run in the other direction?

He racked his brain. He tried to remember all the types of work Violet had covered in the past few years at the DPA.

None had been with children and families. None at all. Had she been avoiding that kind of work?

Other things started to come back. The few things that she'd said in the quiet moments they'd had together.

The fact she hadn't been ready to have a relationship six months ago. Why hadn't she been ready? He'd wanted to press her, had wanted to ask, but it hadn't seemed appropriate.

The fleeting look in her eyes when he'd told her about his friend who worked at Atlanta Memorial. It had the biggest maternity unit in Atlanta.

Was it because she'd had a stillbirth? Was it because she'd had a stillbirth there?

But why would no one know about it? The thought of Violet going through something so heartbreaking made him feel sick.

Was this why he'd never heard of Violet having a relationship in the past three years?

Had she been getting over a stillbirth?

His throat was instantly dry. He couldn't swallow. He'd been in bed with this woman. He'd spent hours in her company.

Why hadn't she told him about this?

He hadn't been able to be around her when he'd thought he was keeping secrets from her. That's what had made him blurt out something he'd kept deep inside for six years.

He'd had to share with her. He'd had to get it off his chest. Because his relationship with Violet hadn't stood a chance without him being honest with her.

So why hadn't she told him anything?

He felt a little fire build inside him. There was more than the personal side here. There was the professional side. He was her team leader.

If a personal event could have affected her ability to do her job out here, he should have known about it.

She should have told him. It should have on her personnel file. Someone should have told him.

Nothing made sense to him.

Hasana was talking to her husband. She was sobbing and obviously tired and distressed.

Her husband looked over toward Violet and didn't hesitate for a second, he held out his hands for his son.

Violet held him out with trembling hands and he took him, putting his arm around his wife and the two of them sat together, crying quietly. He cradled his son, stroking his face then looked at his wife. "Bem." She nodded and put her head on his shoulder as the two of them sat, looking at their child.

Not for Bem the traditional village naming ceremony in seven days' time. His mother and father wouldn't have the usual cause for celebration. But naming their baby was still precious to them, and Violet understood that.

Violet could hear the murmurs of the men

around her. She heard one of them speak to Evan. "His name—it means peace."

Violet stood up moved to the edge of the clearing. She wanted to give them space to grieve together as a family, but she also felt as if she was suffocating.

The darkness and heavy air was closing in around her. She was struggling to breathe and she clawed at the loose *buba* shirt at her neck.

"Violet, what's wrong?" Evan stood in front of her, his wide chest blocking her line of vision. White. He was wearing white. And it cut through the blackness.

His hand touched her cheek, catching a tear with his finger. He pulled her back toward him and cradled her head against his chest, letting her feel the rise and fall of his chest. Her breathing slowed and her panic ebbed. His other reached up and stroked her hair. "You're safe now."

And she did feel safe. It was a relief to finally have some other people around her, to share the burden of being alone in the dark forest with a traumatized patient.

To feel the warmth and strength of someone's

arms around her. But the tightness in her chest was spreading. Sobs rose up in her throat.

She'd just witnessed something very precious. Hasana's husband was grieving for his son as much as she was. He'd held his hands out for his son without hesitation and had looked at him with such tenderness it had broken her heart.

Her daughter had never had that. A father's love. A father to grieve over her. Blane had sent her a simple card when he'd heard the news. He hadn't been there to see how precious their daughter had been. How perfect. How beautiful.

He hadn't touched her little cheek or held her close to his chest.

Not the way Hasana's husband had for their son.

And it hurt. Just when she thought she was moving on, she realized there was something else to regret about her daughter's birth.

Evan lifted her chin so she faced him. His eyes were looking straight at her, illuminated by the torchlight around them. His blue eyes were dark, with the gold flecks standing out in the dim light. There was intensity about them she'd never seen before.

And even though she could see a hundred questions in his eyes he didn't hesitate—he pulled her into his arms and just held her. Held her as if he'd never let her go.

It was as if he knew, for those few seconds, exactly what she needed.

They stood in the darkness like that for a few minutes. She could feel his strong heartbeat beneath his chest. It slowed her and steadied her. Gave her room to breathe. The comfort from his arms felt like the warmest blanket she'd ever been wrapped in.

She wasn't alone in the forest anymore.

His lips brushed the side of her cheek. "Why didn't you tell me, Violet?" he whispered. "Why didn't you tell me about your baby?"

The words caught in her throat. How could he know? How could he know how raw she was feeling? How much she had pent up inside her?

Every muscle in her body was tensed, every hair standing on end.

He looked hurt. He looked upset.

"How, Evan? How can you know that? I haven't told anyone."

He shook his head. "I didn't need you to tell me, Violet." He ran his finger down her cheek.

"It was right here for me to see. I just needed to notice the signs."

The words hung between them and Violet sucked in a breath. She couldn't stand the tension. "What about Urbi, the midwife? How is she? Did they hurt her?" She couldn't stand the thought of that. She couldn't stand the thought they might have hurt the woman who had tried to warn her. Tried to save her.

Evan shook his head. The obvious change of subject must have hurt him. "She'll need some stitches. But she'll be fine. Luke is taking care of her."

The men started to move, to organize themselves to help carry Hasana back to the village. Her husband still stood with his baby in his arms, his head held high.

Evan pulled Violet over to one side. He kept his arm around her. "I don't understand Violet. I don't understand why you didn't tell me. It's such a huge part of your life—so important. Why couldn't you share that with me?"

She shook her head. "I couldn't, Evan. I haven't even told my family."

He looked horrified. "What?"

"You don't understand. My mom and stepdad

are just so frail. After what happened with Saw-yer…" Her voice tailed off and she shook her head again. "Blane and I had decided to split up. I was doing it on my own. They would have been worried sick. And Sawyer, I didn't know how to contact him."

"I can't believe this. I can't believe you had to do this alone. You had *no one* with you?"

"I had a few close girl friends. They were fantastic. I couldn't have asked for more."

"Yes. Yes, you could. You could have asked for a whole lot more." There was an edge of irritation to his voice. Frustration about a situation he'd had no control over.

She sighed. "Nothing like that was meant to happen to me. I hadn't even considered it. I'd had a fairly easy pregnancy and expected to have my baby then let my mom and stepdad know. They would have been delighted. A grandchild would have been the joy to help heal their wound." She couldn't help the wistful tone in her voice.

She'd been hoping for salvation for her family—a new start for them all.

All she'd been left with had been a dark, heart-wrenching hole.

The villagers started to move past them. And they had to follow or be left behind in the forest.

Evan reached down and intertwined his fingers with hers. "There's so much I want to ask you, Violet, but this just doesn't seem like the time or the place." He stretched his other arm in front of them. "We've got a long walk ahead. I want you to tell me. I want you to tell me about your baby."

There was such a calm and determined manner about his words. He made it sound so simple. It was like an open invitation. An open invitation to share her daughter with someone else.

It seemed huge. It seemed enormous. No one had ever asked about her daughter before. How could they, when they hadn't known?

She'd thought she'd put this behind her.

But she'd left the most crucial part of her healing out.

The ability to share.

To share the joy and pain of her daughter.

And now she finally could.

They walked for a long time. She held up her head as they walked through the dark night. She had the strangest feeling around her.

Relief.

Relief to finally talk about her daughter. Yes, she'd spoken with the doctors and the coroner. Yes, she'd spoken with her friends. But her circle of friends had been so small that after a time she'd felt as if she'd had to stop.

This was entirely different. This was a chance to share with someone she cared about.

Loved.

The word shot out of the dark like a bullet to the brain.

Love? Was that how she really felt about Evan?

He was the first thing she thought about in the morning and the last thing in her dreams at night.

She spent the whole day waiting to see his smile or to feel his skin against hers.

Even when she was mad at him, she couldn't stop thinking about him.

The man had well and truly got under her skin.

What was the measure of love, anyway? Because, for her, right now, it felt as if there was only one.

Could she share with him about her daughter? The pain, the terror and the hidden parts of joy?

Yes. Yes, she could.

She squeezed the hand that was holding hers. "My daughter's name was Daisy," she began.

His step faltered then he gave her a smile. "What a beautiful name." He nodded knowingly. "A perfect name for a daughter." They walked for another few steps. "Violet and Daisy. Perfect combination."

She felt a little swell in her heart. A swell of pride that he appreciated the name that had come to her straight away. As soon as they'd told her that her baby was going to be a girl, she'd known exactly what she would call her.

And it felt good to say her name out loud rather than just look at it on a memorial wall. On a little plaque only she visited.

She took a deep breath. This wasn't as hard as she'd thought it would be but, then, she'd been so afraid to do this. Maybe it was all about timing. Or maybe it was all about sharing with the right person.

"She was perfect, Evan. There was nothing wrong with her. Full term. No complications. She had fine blond hair and blue eyes. And her skin… it was perfect." She could see her right then— as if she were right before her eyes. She inhaled deeply, trying to remember her gorgeous baby smell. The silky touch of her unblemished skin. The tiny eyelashes and soft fingernails.

He gave her hand a little squeeze. "She must have taken after her mom, then."

It felt good. He was helping her give Daisy some perspective. Giving Daisy her place in the world as a permanent part of her.

She heard him draw a deep breath. "The perfect part. Was that the hardest? Because I think that would have been the hardest for me." In the dark, his words sounded husky, as if he was struggling to get them out.

Wow. The words that cut right to her heart. The hardest thing of all. It almost took the breath from her lungs. How could he understand like that? Was it the doctor in him—or was it just Evan?

"Yes." Her voice was wavering but she couldn't help it. He understood. He actually *understood* what the hardest part to get over was. "I wanted a reason. I hated being a statistic, a number. I couldn't apportion blame anywhere. It made me think about every single thing I'd ever done during my pregnancy, every single thing I'd ever eaten. Every twinge. Every restless night. There was no one left to put the blame on but myself." She shook her head, her voice drifting off. "It was a normal day. We were planning on a delivery date. It was a routine scan."

She didn't need to say the rest. The horror of there being no heartbeat. The ominous silence in the room. The darting looks between the staff. And the crumpled chart in her hand that revealed her baby's movements. Right up until an hour before.

He released her hand and wrapped an arm back around her shoulders. Then he did something she didn't expect. He pulled her close and walked with his other hand on her belly.

She could feel it. She could feel it all around them. The way he was trying to comfort her. To be there for her. If she believed in auras Evan would have surrounded them in a green healing glow.

She'd thought the walk back through the forest would be long. She'd thought it would be tough. But it felt as if it was passing in the blink of an eye.

This almost felt cathartic to her.

His voice was quiet, just loud enough for them

both to hear it. "I think I would have felt the same. It's the doctor in you, Violet. You look for a rational, reasonable explanation. When the world is full of 'don't knows' it makes it so much more difficult to move on."

He wasn't just talking about her. He was talking about him too.

It was strange. She hadn't seen any similarities in the things they'd had to deal with—probably because they'd never discussed them. Now they seemed crystal clear.

Two entirely different scenarios, one affecting Evan, both affecting her. The individual effects had been devastating.

And they'd both struggled. Someone else understood. For the first time it felt as if someone else understood.

But would he understand what she had to do next?

"I know what you mean, Evan." She looked around her. They were nearing the edge of the forest. The denseness of the trees was diminishing. The foliage was thinning out. Even the darkness was fading a little thanks to the moon, high in the sky.

Their journey was coming to an end.

The men were still carrying Hasana between them. They were a little ahead, starting to weave their way through the houses. Shrieks came from the villagers who spotted them and ran to embrace them in relief that they'd been found.

Almost automatically she could hear the level and tone of the voices changing. Discovering the outcome for Hasana's baby. Then she heard Urbi's voice above the rest—strong and authoritarian, ordering them to take Hasana and her baby to one of the houses. She heard her speaking to some of the men, telling them to prepare the village burial ground. Hasana, along with many of the villagers, was Hausa and would follow the Islamic burial principles. They would bathe and wrap Bem's little body and perform a blessing prior to his burial.

She turned to face him. The burial would take place in a few hours. She wanted to wait for that, but then she had to go. She had to leave.

She reached up and touched his cheek.

"Thank you for finding me, Evan. Thank you for finding *us*."

He knew. He could obviously sense it. The emphasis on that tiny word. He gave her lazy, sexy smile that she loved. "There was always going to be an *us,* Violet. It was written in the stars."

This was going to be so hard.

The hardest thing she'd done in the past three years.

It would be so easy to step into his arms and forget about the day she'd just had. It would be so easy to chalk up everything that just happened to the stress of the moment.

A reaction.

To allow herself to go back to their camp with him and into his bed.

But she had to be true to herself.

She didn't want to stumble on for another few months. Enjoying the days and nights with Evan, knowing that there was an inevitability to their relationship. She didn't want to wait around for the long silences and fights about family.

She had to do this now.

Before the strength left her completely. Her legs were already starting to tremble.

She stared into his eyes and took a deep breath. "You know now, Evan. You know about my daughter. You know about my life." She paused for a second. "And I know about yours." She willed back the tears that were pooling in her eyes. "And now I need to do the hardest thing of all."

His brow furrowed, almost as if a sweep of dread had just come over him. "What is it, Violet? What's wrong?"

She lowered her eyes and laid a hand on his chest. "I can't take the final steps with you around me, Evan. I can't heal. Because you won't let me." He looked as if he wanted to interrupt and she shook her head. "You have to let me finish. And somehow I realize you're not as far along the healing process as I am. You have to find your own way."

She looked around her. "I thought I was ready. I thought I'd waited long enough—kept myself out of harm's way. That's why I spent the past three years hiding in an office at the DPA instead of being out in the field. But being here has taught me that there are still a few steps I have to take."

She lifted her eyes to meet his. It took all her strength to continue. She could already see the panic start to flare in his eyes. "I have to talk to my family. No. I have to *share* with my family. I have to let them grieve for the niece and grand-daughter that they never knew. I have to let them know where I am in this life. I've got to stop thinking about them for a little while. I've got to stop trying to protect them. And I've got to start thinking about me. I need to let them take care of me."

She could feel her voice start to become more determined. She knew this was the only way forward for her. "And I can't deal with your grief and mine. It's too much, Evan. It's too much for one person to take. I thought I needed to get away from you before. Before I came here. Kissing you that night unleashed a whole lot of demons I didn't know how to deal with. I was feeling attracted to someone again. I was feeling lustful."

Her voice dropped. "I wanted to do the kind of things that could get me back in a situation I couldn't control before. But you've helped me. You saw me through that part. I know I can have a relationship again. I know I can feel free to love someone again."

She drew a deep breath.

"But I can't do this with you, Evan. I need to be free. Free to finally move on."

She took a step back and pulled her hand away from his chest. She had to put some distance between them. "You have to take the next step for you. No matter what that might be. And what I really need to do is get away from you. I love you, Evan. But I can't love you like this."

He couldn't hold his tongue any longer. His arms automatically reached out for her and she had to back away. "No, Violet. You don't need to leave. We can work through this together. Whatever you need to do, that's fine with me." He tried to brush his fingers against her cheek. "I'll wait. I'll wait until you're ready."

"You're the one who's not ready, Evan. You're the one who's not ready for me."

She stepped back even further. She had to stay strong. She loved him, but he wasn't ready to be with her.

The sorrow in his eyes was killing her. This was hurting them both. She looked straight into his dark blue eyes. She needed him to understand how far this whole experience had taken her. "Never in a million years did I think I'd end up in this position. I would never have set foot on a plane to Africa if I could ever have imagined this. I knew I would be working with children and families. I knew I would be working with babies. But I thought I was ready. I felt ready. I felt as if I was moving in the right direction."

She threw up her hands. "But a stillborn baby? In the middle of a forest, fleeing from kidnappers? I could never have predicted that. I could never have realized how important to me that could be."

She wanted to leave him with something positive. She couldn't bear the haunted expression on his face.

"This wasn't a bad experience for me, Evan, but it was life-changing. Life-changing in a good way. I'll never see anything like that again. If I'd stayed in Atlanta I would never have been put in that situation. But I was. And I'm glad. Not glad for Hasana and her son but glad that I was able to be there, able to help. Able to understand. Once I've attended Bem's funeral it will be time for me to go back home. It's time for me to make my peace, once and for all."

And then she saw it, the tremble at his throat and the shine of tears in his eyes.

She could only whisper, "Don't make this any

harder, Evan. If you love me as much as I love you, you'll let me do this."

And she turned and walked away before her heart could break all over again.

CHAPTER TWELVE

Two months later

HE WAS WAITING. Waiting in arrivals. His dark hair still shaggy, a baseball cap stuck on his head, wearing a pair of jeans and a pale blue shirt.

He didn't look happy.

Evan heaved his bag over his shoulder and carried his case in his hand, reaching him before he could change his mind and walk away.

"This had better be good. This is the second time in two months someone's asked me to meet them off a plane. Last time didn't go so well."

Sawyer hadn't changed. There was still that animosity between the two of them that had always been there.

"Did you know? Did you know about Violet?"

Evan shook his head. "I had no idea, Matt. Truly, I didn't. I only found out when we were over there."

Sawyer's eyes ran up and down his body then lingered on his face. Obviously trying to decide if he believed him or not. Finally his shoulders sagged a little. "Well, that's okay, then."

He turned toward the exit. "What is it you want to talk about, Evan? We've never exactly been friends."

Evan stomach churned. He wanted to get this over and done with. He should have done this years ago—but Sawyer hadn't been around.

His throat was dry and his mouth parched. Nineteen hours of travel could do that to you.

A red neon sign caught his eye and he said the last words in the world he thought he ever would. "Sawyer, let's get a beer."

Sawyer raised his eyebrow. "Seriously?"

"Seriously."

They waited a few minutes while the bartender got their beers then sat down at a table in the corner of the bar.

"So what's the story with you and Violet?"

Evan felt the hairs stand up on the back of his neck. Sawyer was her brother. It was an obvious question. He took a quick swig from his bottle then put it back down on the table. Maybe he should have waited. Waited until he'd drunk a few more of these before talking to Sawyer. "Nothing. I'm not here to talk about Violet."

"You're not? What do you want to talk about, then?" Sawyer looked confused.

"Helen."

"What?"

He looked across the table at Sawyer. He had the same pale green eyes as his sister. It was kind of disturbing.

"I need to talk to you about Helen."

"You've left it kind of late. It's been six years, Evan."

"I know exactly how long it's been." His words were curter than he'd intended. But he could feel the pressure building in his veins. He had no idea what Matt's reaction would be.

Sawyer's finger was running round the top of his bottle. As if he was trying to decide what to say next.

It was now or never.

"Helen told me she wasn't feeling well."

Sawyer's head shot straight up. "What?"

There was no need for any preamble here.

"That day—of the mission—I was checking

the inventory and Helen said she wasn't feeling one hundred percent."

Sawyer's eyes fixed on the table. "And what did you do?"

There was silence for a few seconds. He'd started now and he had to finish. No matter what the outcome.

"Nothing, Sawyer. I did nothing." His finger traced a circle on the table of the wet outline from his bottle. "I have no excuse. I didn't pick up on it until later. I wasn't paying attention. I didn't remember what she'd said until it was too late."

"And you've waited six years to tell me that?" The tone in his voice was clear.

"I didn't know what to say."

"Sorry would have been a start."

"You think I'm not sorry? You think I haven't gone over and over this in my head? That if I'd stopped and asked Helen more questions that day she might still be here, still be married to you?" His voice was rising and heads were turning in the bar.

He ran his fingers through his hair. "I wish I could turn back time. I wish I could go back to that day and that throw-away comment and *stop*.

Stop and ask her what was wrong, why she didn't feel great. If there was anything else. If there was a possibility that she was pregnant."

Sawyer leaned back in his chair. His fingers hadn't moved from the top of his bottle. "You think you're the only one, Evan? The only one who hasn't gone over that day time and time again, wondering if there was anything different you could have done, different you could have said? Welcome to my life, Evan Hunter." He picked up his bottle and took a long slug.

Evan hesitated. "Violet said…Violet said you had no idea Helen was pregnant." He met Sawyer's eyes. "For a long time I thought you did know. I thought you and Helen might have been keeping the news under wraps. I'm sorry."

Sawyer stared at him for the longest time. "I know. Violet told me." He took off his baseball cap and flung it on the table.

"She told you?"

Sawyer nodded.

"What else did she tell you?"

He shook his head. "Only that. I knew there had to be more to the story. But she only told me that you thought we'd kept you out of the loop. She also told me she put you straight."

Evan felt a little flutter of relief. And he couldn't help the wry smile on his face at the mention of her name.

Sawyer straightened up. "Let me be frank. I agonized over Helen's death for six years. She was the light of my life. My reason to get up every day. When I married Helen I truly believed that we would grow old together. That we would end up with a pair of rockers out on our porch."

Evan smiled. He could almost picture the scene in his head.

He leaned across the table. "The only person I blamed for Helen's death was me, Evan, not you. *I* should have figured out my wife was pregnant. *I* should have stopped her going on that mission. I should have been able to save her. Not you. Not anyone else. Because I was the person she trusted most."

The color was building in his cheeks, the blood obviously pumping in his veins. But he stopped and took a deep breath. "But you know what? It's been six years. And I've got past it. I've had to get past it. Because there's a whole other life out there, Evan. And I know that Helen would have been the first person to tell me that."

Evan listened to the words. Even he could see the change in Sawyer. "Callie?"

Sawyer nodded and took another swig from his bottle. "Callie."

There was an inevitability about all this. A natural way for this conversation to go.

The tightness that had been in his stomach for the past six years was finally starting to unfurl.

"I didn't get it, Evan. I didn't get everyone else's loss. I was selfish. I was too focused on myself. Then I met Callie and my whole world changed." He snapped his fingers. "Just like that. I didn't think I'd ever get the chance of something like that again. I didn't think I'd ever deserve it. Being with Callie has changed everything for me. I've got a reason to get up in the morning again." He paused. There was regret written all over his face.

"When I think about what Violet has gone through on her own I feel so helpless. And so angry at myself. She's my sister. She needed me and I wasn't there."

Evan nodded slowly, raising his eyes. "Kind of angry with you about that myself."

Their eyes met. In quiet understanding.

And they sat for a few moments in silence.

"About Violet..." Evan started.

"Yeah, about Violet," countered Sawyer.

"What are we going to do about that?" The words hung in the air between them.

Sawyer took a final slug of his beer and stood up, stretching his back and sticking his baseball cap back on his head. "Guess you're going to have to stop hating me so much if you're going to be part of the family."

Evan raised his eyebrows. "I've never hated you, Sawyer." He stood up too and threw some bills on the table. "I just never liked you much."

Sawyer threw his head back and let out a laugh. They walked toward the door.

Evan put his hand on Sawyer's arm. "Violet? Where will I find her?"

Sawyer quirked his lip and touched the peak of his cap. "You'll figure it out."

CHAPTER THIRTEEN

VIOLET WALKED SLOWLY along the path. It was another beautiful day in Atlanta. It seemed as though the sun had been shining constantly since she'd got back.

Almost as if something was trying to remind her that she should still be in Africa.

The garden was quiet and she was grateful. The last few times she'd been here her mom and step-father had been with her. They needed time and a place to grieve too, and the memorial garden was probably the most appropriate place.

But she was still trying to adjust. Trying to adjust to sharing her grief with other people. She was used to the calm of the garden, the tranquility. The first few times her mom had come with her it had almost felt like an invasion of her privacy.

Her family was still tiptoeing around her. Even Sawyer. Which was strangely uncomfortable.

She wasn't quite sure if it was what she'd told him or the presence of Callie in his life that was keeping him so even-tempered. But he'd changed. Changed in a good way.

It was good having her brother back in her life. And he was slowly but surely finding a path back into the DPA. Which was just as well, as she'd taken a leave of absence for a while.

The director had been very understanding. He'd told her to take as much time as she needed, had offered her counseling and let her know that any career path within the DPA was open to her.

Violet approached the little granite plaque. It was attached on the wall next to hundreds of others. Sometimes she stood and read them all. But today she was only interested in her own.

She ran her fingers along the letters. Feeling the bumps and outlines beneath the pads of her fingers.

Daisy Connelly.
Born May 16th. Died May 16th.
A little flower lent not given, to bud on earth and bloom in heaven.

There was a lump in her throat—there would always be a lump in her throat when she came here—but today, for the first time, she wasn't crying.

She arranged her flowers in one of the little vases underneath the plaques. There were too many plaques for everyone to have an individual memorial flower vase, so the people who visited had to share.

She always brought the same flowers, a mixture daisies and violets for her daughter from her mommy.

A little array of pink flowers caught her eye with a little white card attached. She couldn't help but peek at the text. *Today I brought you petunias.* They were cute. Obviously hand-picked due to the haphazard way they'd been placed in the vase.

Her eyes looked along the line. There were more of them.

Today I brought you marigolds.
Today I brought you sky-blue pansies.
Today I brought you poppies.
Today I brought you Livingstone daisies.

They were beautiful. Flowers everyday. Were they from a newly bereaved parent?

She could feel the hairs stand up on the back of her neck. And she knew. Instantly.

Her head whipped around and her breath caught in her throat.

Evan.

Sitting on one of the benches. Watching her. Waiting for her.

Her legs were on autopilot. She was standing in front of him before she knew it.

His tan was deeper, his hair lighter, his eyes just as blue as she remembered.

He gave her the smile she loved so much. "Hi." After two months. One word.

"Hi." Her voice croaked. Her fingers itched to reach out and touch him. But she couldn't. Not yet.

"I came to meet Daisy. To talk to her."

She felt her heart squeeze in her chest. "The flowers are from you?"

He nodded.

"But they're so unusual. Where did you find them?"

He gave a little shrug. "My mom has a beautiful garden of flowers. When I told her why I needed them she made sure I had something different every day."

Wow. He'd told his mother about her. She didn't dare to think what that might mean. She counted along the wall. Ten lots of flowers that were obviously from him—some looking a little worse for wear.

She felt a little startled. "You've been coming here for ten days?"

His eyes met hers. "I knew that I'd meet you here eventually. I just had to learn a little patience."

She sat down on the bench next to him. Her eyes fixing on the wall covered in hundreds of individual plaques. So many little lost lives. So many families grieving.

His hand slipped into hers. It felt so natural, his fingers intertwining with hers.

But she held her body rigid. Keeping a wall up around herself.

"When did you get back?"

"Ten days ago."

Ten days. As soon as he'd got back he'd brought some flowers for Daisy.

One of his fingers started tracing a little circle inside the palm of her hand. It was comforting. It was soothing.

"I met your brother."

"What?" Her head shot up.

He nodded slowly. "I called him. Asked him to meet me at the airport." He lifted his eyebrows at her. "We had a beer."

She was imagining this. This couldn't really be happening. This was like one of those crazy dreams that woke you in the middle of the night.

She could feel her heart fluttering in her chest. She squeezed her eyes shut tightly. Maybe she would wake up now and everything would go back to normal.

But all she could feel was the cool summer breeze skittering across her skin.

"Violet?"

She opened her eyes again. The glare from the sun made her blink. She definitely wasn't imagining this.

She was scared to ask. It would have been a showdown between two of the most important men in her life. Surely that couldn't have gone well?

"How did it go?"

She held her breath. Sawyer hadn't said a word to her yesterday. Why not?

"Better than I could have expected. We talked about Helen. Sawyer told me he's tortured himself enough and it's time to move on."

"Oh?" If she held her breath much longer she would burst.

"He mentioned something about being part of the family."

That was it. This must be a dream. This couldn't be happening. She grabbed hold of a little bit of skin and pinched. "Ouch!"

"Violet? What are you doing?"

She jumped up and rubbed her leg. "What do you think I'm doing? I'm pinching myself, trying to work out if this is real."

He stood up next to her and put his hands at her waist. "Oh, it's real all right. Can I do something else to convince you?"

She didn't have time to answer. Because his lips were on hers. Kissing away any doubts. Kissing away any fears.

His warm body was pressing against hers. One hand at the back of her head and the other on her cheek.

"I want to spend the next fifty years convincing you, Violet," he murmured in her ear.

She could feel herself melting. The past two months had been the longest of her life. Working through the grief with her family had been tough. But it was the final act. The final piece of the puzzle.

She wanted to go forward. Go forward and embrace life.

And this was the man she wanted to do it with.

He started kissing around her neck and ears, sending tingles down her spine. "So, this thing with Sawyer, it's over? It's really over?"

His lips moved back to her face, dropping kisses on her nose and eyelids. "It's really over."

A warm wave washed over her. She believed him. She really believed him.

Maybe they could all finally start living their lives again.

She pulled back a little. "Then there's something I want to do."

Her voice was serious and she could see the instant wariness in his face.

She slipped her hand into his and walked back over the wall.

It was time. It was truly time.

She lifted their hands together and placed them on Daisy's plaque.

"Daisy, honey, there's somebody I want you to meet…"

EPILOGUE

"WHAT'S GOING ON? A C-section doesn't take this long." Sawyer paced up and down the corridor.

Callie gave her husband a smile and adjusted the toddler in her lap. "Sit down, honey." She glanced over to where an elderly couple was sitting. "You're making the expectant grandparents nervous."

The doors burst open behind them. *"It's a girl!"*

Evan's face was scarlet, as if he was about to burst with excitement.

Sawyer was up at him in seconds. "Is everything okay? Is she okay? Is Violet okay? What took so long?"

Evan put his hand on Sawyer's arm, his voice steadying as he spoke. "Everything's fine. My wife is beautiful. My daughter is beautiful. Six pounds three ounces, with a perfect Apgar. Her mom's just given her her first feed. I just didn't want to leave their sides. I didn't want to miss a second." He pulled his scrub hat from his head and opened the door behind them. "But now the newest member of the family would like to meet everyone else." He bent down and swooped up the toddler from Callie's lap. "Particularly her big cousin, Riley. Want to see the baby, Riley?"

Riley wrinkled his nose. "Baby," he repeated. "Baby."

Callie laughed and grabbed her husband's hand, holding the door for Sawyer's mom and stepdad. "Let's go, folks. Let's meet the newest family member."

Violet stared down at her daughter. Perfect in every way.

She stroked her finger across her pale skin and downy hair. Leaning forward and taking a deep breath. She just didn't want to let her go.

Evan had been more than an anxious father throughout this pregnancy—even though he'd tried not to show it. In the past few months she'd been scanned every week and when they'd mentioned yesterday that they wanted to deliver her due to the position of her placenta they'd both had a minute of heart failure.

Even though a C-section hadn't been what she'd planned, the most important thing in the world was having a healthy baby.

She dropped more kisses on her daughter's eyelids, watching the rise and fall of her little chest. Moments like these were precious. And all she wanted to do right now was count her blessings.

The doors swung open and the family invasion began.

"She's beautiful!"

"Let me see her!"

"Can I hold her?"

Evan slid on the bed next to her and wrapped his arm around her shoulders. Riley looked at the baby and shuddered. "How are my girls doing?"

She loved it. She loved the way he said it and the tenderness in his eyes.

"We're doing fine." She snuggled against him. "But you were away too long."

She looked up at her family. She could see the tears in her mother's eyes as she leaned over to see her new granddaughter. She could see the relief written across her brother's face.

She watched the smile that he and Callie exchanged as he reached over for his squirming toddler and balanced him on his hip. Becoming a dad suited Sawyer, more than she could ever have imagined.

"Do you have a name?" he asked.

Violet turned to Evan and smiled. "Are you sure it's okay?"

He nodded. "It's beautiful and it suits her perfectly."

Violet turned to her family. "We thought long and hard about a name. I was worried about family traditions." She wrinkled her nose. "Evan's family has a whole host of unusual names. But we've settled on one we both love." She tilted her daughter upward, pulling the blanket down from under her chin. "So, everyone, meet Rose. Rose Hunter. My beautiful daughter."

She smiled as Evan turned to her with a gleam in his eye. "And just think of all the other flowers we've got to choose from."

* * * * *

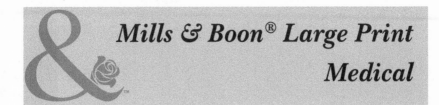

Mills & Boon® Large Print
Medical

June

FROM VENICE WITH LOVE	Alison Roberts
CHRISTMAS WITH HER EX	Fiona McArthur
AFTER THE CHRISTMAS PARTY...	Janice Lynn
HER MISTLETOE WISH	Lucy Clark
DATE WITH A SURGEON PRINCE	Meredith Webber
ONCE UPON A CHRISTMAS NIGHT...	Annie Claydon

July

HER HARD TO RESIST HUSBAND	Tina Beckett
THE REBEL DOC WHO STOLE HER HEART	Susan Carlisle
FROM DUTY TO DADDY	Sue MacKay
CHANGED BY HIS SON'S SMILE	Robin Gianna
MR RIGHT ALL ALONG	Jennifer Taylor
HER MIRACLE TWINS	Margaret Barker

August

TEMPTED BY DR MORALES	Carol Marinelli
THE ACCIDENTAL ROMEO	Carol Marinelli
THE HONOURABLE ARMY DOC	Emily Forbes
A DOCTOR TO REMEMBER	Joanna Neil
MELTING THE ICE QUEEN'S HEART	Amy Ruttan
RESISTING HER EX'S TOUCH	Amber McKenzie